THE
WIND
IN THE
WILLOWS

THE CLASSIC EDITION

THE
Wind
IN THE
Willows

KENNETH GRAHAME

With the original illustrations by

E. H. *Shepard*

Originally published October 8th 1908
by Methuen & Co Ltd
Line illustrations by Ernest H. Shepard
copyright under the Berne Convention
Colouring of the illustrations copyright
© 1970, 1971, Ernest H. Shepard and
Methuen Children's Books Ltd
Text copyright © 1908 Kenneth Grahame

First published in this edition in Great Britain 1998
by Methuen Children's Books
an imprint of Egmont Books Limited
239 Kensington High Street, London W8 6SA
Reprinted in 2001 by Dean, an imprint of Egmont Books Limited.

Introduction © 1998 Brian Sibley
Brian Sibley has asserted his moral rights.

A CIP catalogue record for this book is available
from the British Library

Printed in Spain

Acknowledgements

Thanks are due to the following for
permission to reprint copyright material:
The Bodleian Library for the use of the
portrait of Grahame by John Sargent.
St Edward's School, Oxford, for the use of the portrait of
Kenneth Grahame as a young boy.
The Dorneywood Trust for the studio portrait of
Alastair Grahame by Richard Speaight.
The Estate of E. H. Shepard for the use of
the E. H. Shepard sketches.

Every effort has been made to trace all copyright holders for
material used in "An Honest Book" and the Publishers
apologise if any inadvertent omission has been made.

Contents

"Ratty! Please, I want to row, now!" E. H. Shepard's illustration for the eight colour plate edition published in 1959

"An Honest Book"
by Brian Sibley

"For every honest reader," wrote Kenneth Grahame, "there exist some half-dozen honest books, which he re-reads at regular intervals of six months or thereabouts. Whatever the demands on him, however alarming the arrears that gibber and grin in menacing row, for these he somehow generally manages to find time."

For many honest readers – myself included – *The Wind in the Willows* is just such an honest book. Less of a book, really; more of a good friend with whom you simply must keep in touch, whose company always makes you feel a little more content with life.

That friendship began, for me, when I was nine years old and my parents gave me a thin, pocket-sized edition of the book with small print and without any of Ernest H. Shepard's enchanting illustrations. The only decoration, in fact, was a line drawing, stamped on the pale green cover, of two gnarled trees bending in the wind. Nevertheless – as an only, sickly, child – I fell under the spell of the chattering river and the softly whispering willows. Reading the book in a day, I claimed the characters – gentle-natured Mole, good-hearted Ratty, no-nonsense Badger and the one-and-only, never-to-be-forgotten, utterly outrageous, Mr Toad – for an extended family.

Though lacking the elegance of this present edition, my little copy of *The Wind in the Willows* became one of the best-loved books on my childhood bookshelf. Some of the books that stood alongside it, in those far off days, have long been discarded and forgotten; others are still respected, still capable of evoking affectionate memories, but now seldom read. *The Wind in the Willows*, on the other hand, has remained a constant companion across the changing years.

So what was it about *The Wind in the Willows* that captured my youthful imagination and still captures the fancy of the older, more worldly-wise adult? What I adored, when young, was Kenneth Grahame's ability to spin a yarn full of lovable characters and comic escapades. What fascinates me now, is the daring with which the storyteller interweaves the fun and frolic with episodes of a rare and mystic beauty.

The resulting mix oughtn't to work – indeed, when the book was first published, ninety years ago, in 1908 – a lot of very grown-up people (critics and such like) said that it *didn't* work. Young readers knew better, made the book their own and then persuaded the adults to change their minds.

Like the ancient willow trees that grow along the banks of the Thames and which gave

Kenneth Grahame by John Sargent RA

the book its title, *The Wind in the Willows* has a time-enduring quality. Despite being set in an age that is now two World Wars and numerous social revolutions ago, the book still sells, in its millions, all over the world. Its admirers are legion and include a former President of the United States of America and a good many men of letters including, in our own time, Alan Bennett, and, from an earlier age, A. A. Milne, who once wrote of the book:

> For the last ten or twelve years I have been recommending it. Usually I speak about it at my first meeting with a stranger. It is my opening remark, just as yours is something futile about the weather. If I don't get it in at the beginning, I squeeze it in at the

end. The stranger has got to have it sometime. Should I ever find myself in the dock, and one never knows, my answer to the question whether I have anything to say would be, 'Well, my lord, if I might just recommend a book to the jury before leaving . . .'

As this introduction cannot possibly serve by way of a recommendation – since you wouldn't have bought this handsome new edition unless you already love *The Wind in the Willows*, or want somebody else to love it, or have been told that you are going to love it – I will use the space to tell you something about how this unique and remarkable book came to be written and about the man who wrote it.

Kenneth Grahame was born in Edinburgh, Scotland, on 8 March, 1859, the third child of James Cunningham and Bessie Grahame. His sister, Helen, was aged three; his brother, Thomas William, was just one year old. Cunningham Grahame was a lawyer who, on being appointed Sheriff-Substitute for Argyll, built a grand house for his family, overlooking the loch at Inverary. Kenneth was four years old when, in 1863, the family moved to Inverary. Looking back on his early childhood, Grahame wrote: "The queer thing is, I can remember everything I felt then. The part of my brain I used from four till about seven can never be altered." To Kenneth, everything about life in the new home seemed to be safe and secure. But it was not to be so for long.

The following year, Kenneth's mother gave birth to another son, Roland. A few days later, she fell sick with scarlet fever, then still a life-threatening illness. On 4 April 1864, Bessie Grahame died and, on the same day, Kenneth contracted the disease and was similarly not expected to survive.

Since Kenneth was fighting for his life, the news of his mother's death was kept from him. All the boy knew was that when he was very ill, the one person in the world he most wanted near him, did not come. Eventually recovering, he was told the truth in a coldly clinical way.

A sense of abandonment – first by his mother and then his inconsolable father – forced him towards being solitary and self-reliant. In his later writings, there are scarcely any references to parents and, of the animals in *The Wind in the Willows*, only Otter is married with children.

With his mother's death, Kenneth's life changed out of all recognition. The happy, harmonious environment of the family home in Inverary was shattered.

An inkling of what he lost – and was, thereafter, always seeking – can be glimpsed in an essay, written years later, on the subject of homes: "First there would be a sense of snugness, of cushioned comfort, of home-coming. Next, a gradual awakening to consciousness in a little room, very dear and familiar . . . full of a brooding sense of peace and possession."

An early sketch by E. H. Shepard

No wonder the home would eventually provide such a strong emotional theme in *The Wind in the Willows*. Four very different – but equally desirable – homes are depicted in the book; each of them is loved and cherished and, when parted from, is missed and mourned. Toad's grand mansion; Badger's ancient, ancestral dwelling; Ratty's snug, riverside house; even Mole's friendly little underground home exert a powerful hold on their occupants:

[Mole] saw clearly how plain and simple – how narrow, even – it
all was; but clearly, too, how much it all meant to him, and the
special value of some such anchorage in one's existence. He did
not at all want to abandon his new life . . . but it was good to think
that he had this to come back to, this place which was all his own,
these things which were so glad to see him again and could always
be counted upon for the same simple welcome.

An illustration from the 1959 eight colour plate edition

For young Kenneth, there seemed very little that could be counted upon: his father, a weak man, turned for consolation to the bottle and packed off the new-born baby and the three older children to live with Bessie's mother in Cookham Dene, Berkshire.

Granny Ingles certainly did her duty by Kenneth and his brothers and sister: she raised and educated her daughter's family with little financial assistance from Cunningham Grahame. She was, however, a cold and remote woman who seemed unable to give her grandchildren any real affection. Helen, Thomas and baby Roland adapted to their new life rather better than Kenneth who retreated further into himself and the private worlds of his vivid imagination, of which he wrote, years later, in 1895: "Whenever a child is set down in a situation that is distasteful, out of harmony, jarring, that very moment he begins without conscious effort to throw out and to build up an environment really suitable to his soul, and to transport himself thereto . . ."

For Kenneth, there was much in his new surroundings to offer escape into a private kingdom of his own. "These kingdoms," he later wrote, "exist side by side with the other life, occupying at least a fair half of actual existence, always there, always handy to step into . . ."

Granny Ingles' house, "The Mount", was an idealised country cottage – once a hunting lodge – with roses round the door and the leaded windows, flowering creepers climbing towards the tiled eaves and a large upstairs room, called the Gallery, which the children were allowed to commandeer and which, for them, became "an imaginary city". Beyond the house, its gardens and orchard, was Quarry Wood – the inspiration for the Wild Wood – and the water meadows that ran down to the river with its reeds and osiers and its stooping willow trees trailing their leaves in the meandering Thames.

Kenneth may have yearned for the affection which Granny Ingles seemed incapable of giving and – with his father's move to Le Havre, in France – felt the pain of the final break with the old memories of happiness and stability, but there were plenty of new joys: exploring, inventing, imagining; getting to know the different trees and plants, being able to identify the birds and animals that inhabited wood, field and river bank.

Sometimes he was joined by his brother and sister, but often he was on his own, establishing, without realizing it, the lifelong characteristics of "the loner". It is interesting that each of the central characters in *The Wind in the Willows* – despite shared picnics and boating expeditions – are, essentially, loners who, even when living together, require times of undisturbed solitude.

Grahame's passion for the river – always changing, always the same – is eloquently expressed in the pleasure which the Water Rat derives from "simply messing about in boats". And, in his description of Mole's encounter with the river, early in *The Wind in the Willows*, we see, perhaps, a personal recollection from those childhood days in Cookham Dene:

> All was a-shake and a-shiver – glints and gleams and sparkles,
> rustle and swirl, chatter and bubble. The Mole was bewitched,
> entranced, fascinated. By the side of the river he trotted as
> one trots, when very small, by the side of a man who holds one
> spellbound by exciting stories . . .

Just as the author of those words has held generations of readers spellbound: telling them stories, granting them glimpses into those secret kingdoms, originally created for his own private escape.

Long after childhood, Grahame's love of the natural world enabled him to depict it fancifully – yet, at the same time, truthfully; and he remained, for ever, at one with nature. His friend, the artist Graham Robertson, recalled how, in later years, when they were walking together: "He would slowly become part of the landscape and a word from him would come as unexpectedly as a sudden remark from an oak or a beech."

The days at Cookham Dene were happy, but short-lived. Granny Ingles and the young Grahames moved a few miles away to Cranbourne around the time that Kenneth turned seven – after which, he later said, he "did not remember anything particularly." A childhood first cursed by the sharp, inexplicable pain of separation from parents and home, and then blessed by the discovery of a new, inner world of the imagination, made Grahame what he was: in one sense eternally the child aged between four and seven, ill-equipped to face many of the vicissitudes of life; but well-gifted to speak to children with the authentic voice of youth and to awaken the childhood memories of grown-ups.

In 1868, Kenneth was sent to school at St Edward's, Oxford. Being, as he put it, a "small school-boy, newly kicked out of his nest into the draughty,

uncomfortable outer world", he fell prey to the usual tortures of public school life. Nevertheless, he did well at his studies and at sport and became Head of School. He also fell under the spell of the city of dreaming spires, the "good grey Gothic" buildings and "the cool, secluded reaches of the Thames . . . remote and dragon-fly haunted".

Kenneth Grahame at school

He hoped that he might be allowed to continue at Oxford and study at one of the colleges, but Granny Ingles was adamant: the boy must go out into the wide world and work

for his living, and a clerkship was secured for him at the Bank of England. Having to wait three and half years before he could take up the post, he entered the office of one of his uncles, who was a parliamentary agent.

Years later, Grahame had Toad sing: "The clever men at Oxford know all there is to be knowed, but none of them know one half as much as intelligent Mr Toad"; but the bitter disappointment at being denied an Oxford education never left him. However, being – like Mole – a hopeful creature, keen to look for the best in any situation, Grahame found much about his new life in the City to engage his imagination and emotions: particularly the sense of place, the colour and texture of daily life in the soot-stained streets where "buses whirl up and recede in vivid spots of red and green".

From a child, Grahame's strongest feelings had always been for places rather than for people who could desert you, let you down or simply fail to love you. Years later he remarked to his wife: "You *like* people, they interest you. But I am interested in places." And repeatedly in *The Wind in the Willows*, Grahame's fascination with place comes through: the detailed descriptions of the  animal's houses – grand, humble, majestic or cosy; the picturesque portraits of the river in its varied moods; the romantic vision of faraway lands that only a bold wayfarer might visit; or, nearer to home, the way in which the winter snows transform the terrors of the Wild Wood into a wonderland of "snow-castles and snow-caverns".

Using a ledger – such as he worked with every day in his office – Grahame began jotting down the scenes he saw, sketching the characters he met, considering the ways of the world. He was on the way to discovering his true vocation: not that of the Oxford scholar which he longed to be, nor the city businessman that others wanted him to be, but an observer and chronicler of life. A writer.

Although he was still regretting missed opportunities, Grahame began an education of a kind he could never have acquired at Oxford. By the time he took up his post at the Bank of England, in 1879, he was a member of several literary societies, and had met many of the leading men of letters of his day, among them Tennyson, Browning, Ruskin and William Morris.

Grahame's first article was published in the *St James's Gazette* on Boxing Day, 1888, and he was soon contributing to other publications including the *National Observer*, where his essays and sketches were quickly noticed – especially since they appeared alongside contributions from W. B. Yeats, H. G. Wells, J. M. Barrie, Thomas Hardy and Rudyard Kipling.

In 1893, John Lane published – under the title *Pagan Papers* – a collection of Grahame's magazine pieces, among them "The Rural Pan", with its early incarnation of "The Piper at the Gates of Dawn":

> . . . In solitudes such as this, Pan sits and dabbles, and all the air is full of the music of his piping . . . Out of hearing of all the clamour, the rural Pan may be found stretched on Ranmore Common, loitering under Abinger pines, or prone by the secluded stream of the sinuous Mole, abounding in friendly greetings for his foster-brothers the dab-chick and the water rat . . .

And not just Pan, but a Water Rat and (though it is here the name of a river) a Mole . . .

Pagan Papers also introduced Harold, a young hero – modeled, in part, on the author – who demonstrated an aptitude for getting round tiresome rules and regulations that was later inherited by Toad. Locked up in his room all day for some misdemeanour, Harold "had very soon escaped by the window . . . and had only gone back in time for his release".

More stories featuring Harold and other child characters were published first in the *National Observer* and then in *The Yellow Book*, before being collected into book form as *The Golden Age* (1895) and *Dream Days* (1898), two books which earned their author considerable fame and established his reputation. Reviewers described the books as "every reader's autobiography", and one critic went so far as to say: "It matters little whether or not Mr Grahame writes any more . . . he has given us a four-square piece of literature, complete in itself."

Maybe Grahame took the compliment too literally, for it was to be a full decade before he wrote another book, the one for which he is now remembered, *The Wind in the Willows*.

He preferred to think of any creative impulses he had as being "a spring" rather than "a pump" and, even when the muse was upon him, found the actual inky business of writing an enormous effort: "There is always a pleasure in the exercise; but, also, there is always agony in the endeavour."

Also, unlike many writers, he didn't have to write for money, especially since in 1898, the year which saw the publication of *Dream Days*, Grahame was appointed to the post of Secretary of the Bank of England. One of the youngest men to hold this office, Grahame was just 39 and, to some of those who knew him, looked younger: "He had," said one acquaintance, "a startled air and seemed to be a man who had not become quite accustomed to the discovery that he was no longer a child."

The duties of Bank of England Secretary were not so onerous as to prevent his finding a few hours to work at his ledger of stories; but his life took another, unexpected, turn of events when, in 1899, he married an admirer and sometime writer, Elspeth Thomson.

Many of those closest to Grahame were astonished at the marriage since he had seemed a confirmed bachelor whose life was regulated on similar easy-going lines to those observed by Rat, Mole, Toad and Badger who were, to a man, unencumbered by the female of the species – except, of course, for possible dealings with the occasional washerwoman!

In 1900, the Grahames had a son whom they christened Alastair, but who was always known as "Mouse". Born prematurely, the child was blind in one eye and had a bad squint in the other. The parents doted on their Mouse: Kenneth attempting to give the boy those things that he felt had been missing from his own childhood; Elspeth attempting to ignore Alastair's disability and convince herself (and everyone else – including the boy) that he was a child genius.

It was a recipe for disaster. Badly spoilt, Mouse developed ungovernable mood swings: sometimes arrogant and unruly; sometimes insecure and depressed; always demanding. Much of Mouse's disturbing personality – especially his often violent temper tantrums – were to be immortalized in the character of Toad who is, at one moment, reckless and boastful and, at the next, crushed and contrite. Indeed, it is to Mouse that we owe not just the characterization of Mr Toad, but the very creation of *The Wind in the Willows*.

An effective way of calming Mouse's bad moods was for his Daddy to tell him a story and that is what happened on the night of his fourth birthday: "He had a bad crying fit," Grahame wrote to a friend, "and I had to tell him stories about moles, giraffes and water rats (he selected these as his subjects) till after 12."

The bedtime story begun on that stressful birthday continued to be told over a period of three years, during which Mouse was aged from four to seven – the very years that had been so important to the young Kenneth.

The water rat remained in the story, but the giraffe was soon replaced by another animal. "I remember," Elspeth Grahame was to write, "on asking my maid to tell Kenneth that we were already very late in starting for some dinner-party, that she mentioned: 'Oh, he's up in the night-nursery, telling Master Mouse some ditty or other about a toad'."

Portrait of Alastair Grahame by Richard Speaight

When, in 1906, the Grahames decided to move to the country, Kenneth chose to return to the place of his short-lived childhood happiness: Cookham Dene, in Berkshire. Their new country home – once again near the beloved river – provided fresh inspiration for Grahame's nightly storytelling that, one evening, was overheard by a house-guest whose account of her eavesdroppings was romantically written-up by Elspeth in her 1944 book, *First Whisper of "The Wind in the Willows"*:

> It sounded like music, and every word slid just into its rightful
> place. There was magic in it, there was sense in it, and above all
> there was beauty in it . . . I know there was a Badger in it, a Mole,
> a Toad, and a Water Rat, and the places they lived in and were
> surrounded by.

When, the following year, Mouse went to the seaside without his parents, Kenneth continued the story in a series of letters, thoughtfully preserved by the child's governess and returned to Mrs Grahame. The first of these letters takes up the tale of Toad well into the story as we know it, and follows an episode that was never incorporated into the book:

> My darling Mouse,
> Have you heard about the Toad? He was never taken prisoner by
> brigands at all. It was all a horrid low trick of his. He wrote that
> letter himself – the letter saying that a hundred pounds must be
> put in the hollow tree. And he got out of the window early one
> morning, & went off to a town called Buggleton, & went to the
> Red Lion Hotel & there he found a party that had just motored
> down from London, & while they were having breakfast he went

into the stable-yard & found their motor-car & went off in it without even saying Poop-poop! And now he has vanished & everyone is looking for him, including the police. I fear he is a very bad low animal.

Goodbye, from

Your loving Daddy

Which is roughly where we find Toad halfway through Chapter 6 of the published book.

To begin with, the letters (there were fifteen in all) began in a racy style, lacking the detail and description found in the book and serving more as a series of news bulletins on Toad's exploits: "No doubt you have met some of the animals & have heard about Toad's Adventures since he was dragged off to prison by the bobby & the constable . . ."

The immediacy of Grahame's storytelling is reflected in the way in which the letters conclude: at first with such remarks as "This is as far as I have heard at present", and later with the blatant cliff-hanger device of "To be continued". There are one or two differences between the letters and the book (on the canal, for example, Toad encounters a Bargee not a Barge-woman) but the events are much the same. The letters – which run from May until September, 1907 – gradually become longer and fuller and it is clear, by the seventh, that the writer was well into his stride and had no need for any preliminaries: "Well! So when Toad had stuffed as much breakfast inside of him as he could possibly hold, he stood up, and shook hands with the Gipsy . . ."

The adventures of Toad might have remained an unfinished domestic entertainment, had it not been for the intervention of Constance Smedley, the European agent for the popular American magazine, *Everybody's*. When Miss Smedley – who lived not far from the Grahames, in Bray – asked the author if he would write something for *Everybody's*, he declined; undaunted, she suggested he make a book out of the "unending story", that Grahame nightly recounted to Mouse, "dealing with the adventures of the little animals whom they met in their river journeys."

Even though the stories were related, as Miss Smedley recorded, "in a bedtime visit of extreme secrecy", she seems to have been privy to their telling – or at least to their content – for she observed that "Mouse's own tendency to exult in his exploits was gently satirized in Mr Toad, a favourite character who gave the juvenile audience occasion for some slightly self-conscious laughter". Eventually,

Grahame agreed to attempt a book based on the stories and letters, a difficult undertaking since the early episodes only existed as memories.

While re-working the saga of Toad, Grahame wrote *Bertie's Escapade*, a short story for Alastair about Bertie, a black Berkshire pig who escapes from his pen, just before Christmas, and goes carol singing with two rabbits, named Peter and Benjie. Eventually published in 1944, and illustrated by E. H. Shepard five years later, *Bertie's Escapade* includes an encounter with a Mole – *another* mole – who is employed as a lift-attendant at the nearby Chalkpit Hill and a late-night feast (raided from "Mr Grahame's" larder) of cold chicken, tongue, pressed beef, ginger beer, soda-water and other delights that recall the contents of Ratty's famous luncheon-basket.

The story of *The Wind in the Willows* grew in the writing: Toad's daredevil exploits followed their original desperate course, but Grahame's prose took

*E. H. Shepard's illustrations for **Bertie's Escapade***

on new subtlety of purpose, with exquisitely descriptive passages, such as the Rat's recollections of "the pageant of the river bank" with all its pleasures:

> The languorous siesta of hot midday, deep in green undergrowth, the sun striking through in tiny golden shafts and spots; the boating and bathing of the afternoon, the rambles along dusty lanes and through yellow cornfields; and the long, cool evening at last, when so many threads were gathered up, so many friendships rounded, and so many adventures planned for the morrow.

Whole new episodes – soulful and mystical – were woven into the tapestry. Some readers view the encounter with "The Piper at the Gates of Dawn" (which links the told stories with the Mouse letters) and the Water Rat's meeting with the Seafaring Rat (inspired by Grahame's own expeditions in search of southern sun) as blemishes on the story, others as emotional highlights. Whatever the verdict, the result is a round of changing moods: hilarious madcap adventures interspersed by lyrical, reflective passages.

Although the book's characters had been strongly delineated in the original letters, they gained stature in the re-writing, with Grahame drawing on a variety of inspirations from yachting friends encountered during holidays on the river Fowey (a co-source, with the Thames, of the River in the book) and, in the case of Toad, a dash of that Shakespearean braggart, Sir John Falstaff. The characters – strong, sensible, sensitive or silly – are introduced to us through the eyes of the naïve, innocent Mole. It is Mole, not Toad, who is the book's true central character – for Mole is *us*. As a reader, we do not need to know the ways of the countryside, appreciate the joys of life on the river, or understand why one needs to be careful of the Wild Wood and even more so of the wide world beyond. We learn and discover those things – and many others – in company with Mole.

Mole is also the only character in the book who evolves: maturing from the shy, unsure, nervous creature who, at the beginning, hesitantly steps into Ratty's boat, into the devisor of an ingenious plan which, at the end, helps bring about the downfall of the Wild Wooders.

As for the others, they are too set in their ways: Rat would always be messing about on the river; Badger would, inevitably, return to his reclusive existence and as Grahame confessed, years after writing the book: "Of course Toad never really reformed; he was by nature incapable of it".

When the book was finally completed, it was dispatched to *Everybody's* – who turned it down! So did several British publishers, before it was accepted – somewhat reluctantly – by Methuen.

The American publisher, Charles Scribner only took the book on the recommendation of President Roosevelt who had been sent a copy of the British edition and wrote to the author: "I have read it and re-read it, and have come to accept the characters as old friends."

The book was originally entitled *The Wind in the Reeds* and this explains the references to Mole listening at the reed-stems for "something of what the wind went whispering so constantly among them". However, this title was thought too similar to a book of verse by W. B. Yeats, *The Wind Among the Reeds*, so Grahame offered an alternative, *Mr Mole and His Mates*, which was also rejected. He then considered a string of other possibilities – among them *The Babble of the Stream*, *River Folk* and *The Children of Pan* – before amending his first title to *The Wind in the Willows*.

The book was published on 8 October, 1908, its only illustration being a curious frontispiece by the author's friend, Graham Robertson, showing three naked children sitting by a waterfall (a water rat and an otter just in evidence) with the inscription: "And a River went out from Eden". Maybe this decoration contributed to the apparent confusion among the critics who did not review the book at all favourably.

Punch (with singular lack of humour) described it as "a sort of irresponsible holiday story in which the chief characters are woodland animals, who are represented as enjoying most of the advantages of civilization". *The Times Literary Supplement* observed that "as a contribution to natural history the work is negligible" and complained that a water rat would "never use a boat to navigate a stream" and pondered on the subject of a mole doing whitewashing: "No doubt moles like their abodes to be clean; but whitewashing? Are we very stupid or is this joke really inferior?"

There had been many stories published about animals who dress and act like humans (for example, in the books of Beatrix Potter, the stories of Brer Rabbit and the tales of Oz and Wonderland) but the chief problem was perhaps the fact that Grahame's characters appear to change size, even nature, at will; to be caught up in what one commentator has described as "shifting planes of reality". Mr Toad lives in a baronial hall, drives a motor-car, is tried in a human court of law, imprisoned in a gaol and disguises himself in the clothes of a washerwoman; yet, a few chapters later, he is seized by fore-leg and hind-leg and thrown into the river for being "a horrid nasty, crawly Toad!" Similar descriptive problems arise with all the characters and the reader has simply to accept them for what they are or be constantly perplexed. One contemporary reviewer, Richard Middleton, writing in *Vanity Fair*, wisely noted: "When all is said the boastful, unstable Toad, the hospitable Water Rat, the shy, wise, childlike Badger, and the Mole with his pleasant habit of brave boyish impulse, are neither animals nor men, but are types of that deeper humanity which sways us all."

A. A. Milne, in the introduction to *Toad of Toad Hall*, his play-version of the book, put it this way:

> In reading the book, it is necessary to think of Mole, for instance, sometimes as an actual mole, sometimes as such a mole in human clothes, sometimes as a mole grown to human size, sometimes walking on two legs, sometimes on four. He is a mole, he isn't a mole. What is he? I don't know. And, not being a matter of fact person, I don't mind. At least I do know, and still I don't mind. He is a fairy, like so many immortal characters in fiction; and, as a fairy, he can do, or be, anything.

To the young readers who quickly earmarked the book as their special property – the problem simply did not exist: "It is the special charm of the child's point of view," Grahame wrote, years afterwards, "that the dual nature of these characters does not present the slightest difficulty to them. It is only the old fogies who are apt to begin 'Well, but . . . ' and so on. To the child it is all entirely natural and as it should be."

Despite the uncertainty of the early critics, the first edition of *The Wind in the Willows* sold quickly and was reprinted before Christmas 1908, and three times during the following year.

Among the distinguished writers who had puzzled over the book when it appeared were Arnold Bennett and Arthur Ransome, but other literary men were to become loyal supporters of the book. C. S. Lewis, the chronicler of Narnia, commented that "the child who has once met Mr Badger has got ever afterwards, in its bones, a knowledge of humanity and English history which it certainly couldn't get from any abstraction".

As for A. A. Milne, who would go on to create Winnie-the-Pooh and friends, the book offered repeated opportunities to write in its praise:

> One does not argue about *The Wind in the Willows.* The young
> man gives it to the girl with whom he is in love, and if she does
> not like it, asks her to return his letters. The older man tries it on
> his nephew, and alters his will accordingly. The book is a test of
> character . . . When you sit down to it, don't be so ridiculous as
> to suppose that you are sitting in judgement on my taste, or on
> the art of Kenneth Grahame. You are merely sitting in judgement
> on yourself. You may be worthy: I don't know. But it is you who
> are on trial . . .

By 1929, when Milne adapted the book for the stage – wisely keeping in the fun and games, but leaving out all the wistful, mysterious passages – *The Wind in the Willows* was established as a modern classic. First staged in 1930, *Toad of Toad Hall* became an annual Christmas favourite for many years and is one of the few plays by Milne to survive his lifetime. The book has since been the subject of various dramatic and musical versions, notably Alan Bennett's highly acclaimed adaptation for London's National Theatre, first staged in 1990, which caught more of the diverse aspects of the book than any other dramatization.

The Wind in the Willows has been filmed several times: notably in 1949 by Walt Disney, as a bright and breezy animated romp with a lot of style but only a modicum of faithfulness to the original; in 1983, by the British model animation studio, Cosgrove Hall, using puppets that perfectly captured the characters' combination of animal behaviour and human nature; and, in 1996 by *Monty Python's* Terry Jones, who also played a deliciously extravagant Toad to Eric Idle's Rat, Steve Coogan's Mole and Nicol Williamson's Badger.

The problem of realizing the characters on stage or screen is one which, initially, was shared by illustrators of the book. Kenneth Grahame was opposed to the book being illustrated, believing that it could not be done: how was any artist supposed to depict a scene in which a Toad rides on the footplate of a steam engine – especially when, according to the author, the Toad was train-size and the train Toad-size? However, since the book's growing reputation seemed to demand the addition of pictures, various artists tried their hand.

First, in 1913, was Paul Branson, who produced competent drawings of animals and riverside settings, but who failed to capture the personalities with which Grahame endowed his characters. Next came Nancy Barnhart, who, in 1922, produced a dull, graceless series of pictures featuring lumpen animal figures who could never have danced a jig in the snow or jumped off all four legs at once in the joy of living. Then, in 1927, came Wyndham Payne who adopted a facetious line that ignored the characters' animal shapes and presented them simply as humans with grotesque animal masks. Grahame disliked all these versions, complaining: "My animals are not puppets. They always turn them into puppets." It was not a happy heritage.

Frontispiece by Nancy Barnhart

It was in 1931, that Methuen had the sense to ask Ernest H. Shepard to illustrate the book. A superb illustrator, always sensitive to the mood of the text, Shepard had made his name, in 1924, with his illustrations for the first of A. A. Milne's children's books, *When We Were Very Young*. His illustrations for the following volumes – *Winnie-the-Pooh*, *The House at Pooh Corner* and *Now We Are Six* – had shown him capable of depicting a combination of characters – toys and real animals – as unlikely as those in *The Wind in the Willows*, and placing them in settings which captured a genuine sense of landscape.

At the same time as he was illustrating the exploits of Milne's Bear of Very Little Brain, Shepard was making new pictures for Grahame's earlier books *The Golden Age* (1928) and *Dream Days* (1930). However, when he came to approach Grahame's tale of the river bank, Shepard was far less confident. "There are certain books," he wrote some twenty years later, "that should never be illustrated . . . and I had felt that *The Wind in the Willows* was one of these. Perhaps if it had not already been done, I should not have given way to the desire to do it myself . . ."

Before embarking on the project, Shepard went to visit the author, now an old man: "Not sure about this new illustrator of his book, he listened patiently while I told him what I hoped to do. Then he said, 'I love these little people, be kind to them.' Just that . . ." Grahame went on to tell Shepard where to find the various locations in the story:

> He told me of the river nearby, of the meadows where Mole broke ground that spring morning, of the banks where Rat had his house, of the pools where Otter hid, and of the Wild Wood way up on the hill above the river, a fearsome place but for the sanctuary of Badger's home, and of Toad Hall. He would like, he said, to go with me to show me the river bank that he knew so well, '. . . but now I cannot walk so far and you must find your way alone'.

So the artist went alone, sketching the real locations that Grahame had in mind when writing the story, and gathering as he went his own inspiration:

I poked and pried along the river bank to find where was Rat's
boat house, and where Mole had crossed the river to join him,
and, as I listened to the river noises, the little plops and ripples
that mean so much to the small people, I could almost fancy that
I could see a tiny boat pulled up among the reeds.

An early sketch by E.H. Shepard

The resulting black and white line illustrations – a combination of airy grace
and disciplined draughtsmanship – succeeded in conjuring the atmosphere of the
turning seasons in the Berkshire countryside around Ratty's beloved river. As with
Shepard's illustrations for the *Pooh* books, the authenticity of the settings gives his
pictures a vibrant realism that is intuitively recognized by the reader as being true
and honest.

Without ever losing sight of the characters' animal nature, Shepard deals easily with the difficult issue of scale and size: Mole sitting under the dock-leaves, is mole-sized: picnicking with rat under the willows, he is human-sized; attempting to catch Toad's horse, he is somewhere in-between. The scene outside the back door to Toad Hall effortlessly establishes scale: the door itself is human height, the knocker, letter-box and bell-pulls are at a height convenient for an animal.

Many artists have since revisited the willow-fringed river – among them John Worsley, Eric Kincaid, Les Morrill, Michael Hague, Harry Hargreaves and Paul Hogarth – but none of them have seriously challenged Shepard's interpretation.

Not even the most famous book illustrator of his age, Arthur Rackham, with his assured line and delicate water-colour washes, could do better.

When Shepard had completed his drawings, he took them to show Kenneth Grahame: "Though critical, he seemed pleased and, chuckling, said, I'm glad you've made them real." As indeed he had.

E. H. Shepard

With scarcely a misreading of the text, Shepard captures all the book's disparate charms. Almost thirty years later, the artist revisited the river bank, painting a set of eight colour plates for the 1959 edition; and, in 1969 – when Shepard was almost ninety – he added gem-like colours to his original line illustrations to make the sparkling illustrations newly reproduced for this special edition.

Every reader will have a favourite picture: it might be Rat and Mole exploring the garden at Mole End; or lingering outside the lighted cottage window in the village ("the little curtained world within walls – the larger stressful world of

outside Nature shut out and forgotten"); or, perhaps, Toad the terror, swaggering down his front steps towards his latest motor-car; or Mole struggling along through snow and wind, deep dark shadows looming among the trees at dusk, the only light coming from the dull brilliance of snow among the tree-roots. As the writer Eleanor Graham has observed: "Shepard's pen and the author's might have been dipped in the same inkwell."

An early sketch by E. H. Shepard

At the time of Shepard's final visit, Kenneth and Elspeth Grahame were living near the river in Pangbourne. Grahame had retired from the Bank of England in 1908 and moved to Blewbury, near Didcot, two years later. In 1920, the couple were dealt a sad blow when their son, Alastair, then a student at Christ Church, Oxford, was killed in an accident on a railway line.

The coroner's verdict was accidental death, but the evidence at the time, and the belief of many of those who knew the family, was that the frequently troubled and unhappy Mouse (who as a child, with Toad-like abandon, had lain down in the road when he heard an approaching motor-car) was very probably responsible for his own death.

In 1924, the grief-stricken parents moved to Pangbourne, where Grahame spent his last years an almost total recluse, re-entering those secret worlds, those private retreats, that he had created for himself in childhood.

There were numerous requests for another book; but Grahame always courteously declined. Even his great admirer A. A. Milne who suggested a sequel to *The Wind in the Willows* – "a second wind" – could not change his mind. Although, in recent years, other hands have written several new tales about the characters, they simply cannot compare with the inimitable original.

Those who met Kenneth Grahame in his last years and who had the rare opportunity of talking with him (for he was as shy and retiring as old Badger) might hear him speak his simple, naturalist's philosophy:

> Every animal, by instinct, lives according to his nature. Thereby he lives wisely, and betters the tradition of mankind. No animal is ever tempted to belie his nature. No animal, in other words, knows how to tell a lie. Every animal is honest. Every animal is straight-forward. Every animal is true – and is, therefore, according to his nature, both beautiful and good. I like most of my friends among the animals more than I like most of my friends among mankind.

It can also be truly said of Kenneth Grahame, who died peacefully on 6 July 1932, that he, too, lived wisely and bettered the tradition of mankind – and never more so than with this hauntingly beautiful, boisterously funny book which you are now holding in your hands . . .

Brian Sibley, 1998

Kenneth Grahame

Chapter 1

The River Bank

The Mole had been working very hard all the morning, spring-cleaning his little home. First with brooms, then with dusters; then on ladders and steps and chairs, with a brush and a pail of whitewash; till he had dust in his throat and eyes, and splashes of whitewash all over his black fur, and an aching back and weary arms. Spring was moving in the air above and in the earth below and around him, penetrating even his dark and lowly little house with its spirit of divine discontent and longing. It was small wonder, then, that he suddenly flung down his brush on the floor, said "Bother!" and "O blow!" and also "Hang spring-cleaning!" and bolted out of the house without even waiting to put on his coat. Something up above was calling him imperiously, and he made for the steep little tunnel which answered in his case to the gravelled carriage-drive owned by animals whose residences are near to the sun and air. So he scraped and scratched and scrabbled and scrooged, and then he scrooged again and scrabbled and scratched and scraped, working busily with his little paws and muttering to himself, "Up we go! Up we go!" till at last, pop! his snout came out into the sunlight, and he found himself rolling in the warm grass of a great meadow.

"This is fine!" he said to himself. "This is better than whitewashing!" The sunshine struck hot on his fur, soft breezes caressed his heated brow, and after the seclusion of the cellarage he had lived in so long the carol of happy birds fell on his dulled hearing almost like a shout. Jumping off all his four legs at once, in the joy of living and the delight of spring without its cleaning, he pursued his way across the meadow till he reached the hedge on the further side.

"Hold up!" said an elderly rabbit at the gap. "Sixpence for the privilege of passing by the private road!" He was bowled over in an instant by the impatient and contemptuous Mole, who trotted along the side of the hedge chaffing the other rabbits as they peeped hurriedly from their holes to see what the row was about. "Onion-sauce! Onion-sauce!" he remarked jeeringly, and was gone before they could think of a thoroughly satisfactory reply. Then they all started grumbling at each other.

"How *stupid* you are! Why didn't you tell him –" "Well, why didn't *you* say –" "You might have reminded him –" and so on, in the usual way: but, of course, it was then much too late, as is always the case.

It all seemed too good to be true. Hither and thither through the meadows he rambled busily, along the hedgerows, across the copses, finding everywhere birds building, flowers budding, leaves thrusting – everything happy, and progressive, and occupied. And instead of having an uneasy conscience pricking him and whispering "Whitewash!" he somehow could only feel how jolly it was to be the only idle dog among all these busy citizens. After all, the best part of a holiday is perhaps not so much to be resting yourself, as to see all the other fellows busy working.

He thought his happiness was complete when, as he meandered aimlessly along, suddenly he stood by the edge of a full-fed river. Never in his life had he seen a river before – this sleek, sinuous, full-bodied animal, chasing and chuckling, gripping things with a gurgle and leaving them with a laugh, to fling itself on fresh playmates that shook themselves free, and were caught and held

again. All was a-shake and a-shiver – glints and gleams and sparkles, rustle and swirl, chatter and bubble. The Mole was bewitched, entranced, fascinated. By the side of the river he trotted as one trots, when very small, by the side of a man who holds one spellbound by exciting stories; and when, tired at last, he sat on the bank, while the river still chattered on to him, a babbling procession of the best stories in the world, sent from the heart of the earth to be told at last to the insatiable sea.

As he sat on the grass and looked across the river, a dark hole in the bank opposite, just above the water's edge, caught his eye, and dreamily he fell to considering what a nice snug dwelling-place it would make for an animal with few wants and fond of a bijou riverside residence, above flood level and remote

from noise and dust. As he gazed, something bright and small seemed to twinkle down in the heart of it, vanished, then twinkled once more like a tiny star. But it could hardly be a star in such an unlikely situation; and it was too glittering and small for a glow-worm. Then, as he looked, it winked at him, and so declared itself to be an eye; and a small face began gradually to grow up round it, like a frame round a picture.

A little brown face, with whiskers.

A grave round face, with the same twinkle in its eye that had first attracted his notice.

Small neat ears and thick silky hair.

It was the Water Rat!

Then the two animals stood and regarded each other cautiously.

"Hullo, Mole!" said the Water Rat.

"Hullo, Rat!" said the Mole.

"Would you like to come over?" inquired the Rat presently.

"Oh, it's all very well to *talk*," said the Mole, rather pettishly, he being new to a river and riverside life and its ways.

The Rat said nothing, but stooped and unfastened a rope and hauled on it; then lightly stepped into a little boat which the Mole had not observed. It was painted blue outside and white within, and was just the size for the two animals; and the Mole's whole heart went out to it at once, even though he did not yet fully understand its uses.

The Rat sculled smartly across and made fast. Then he held up his fore-paw as the Mole stepped gingerly down. "Lean on that!" he said. "Now then, step lively!" and the Mole to his surprise and rapture found himself actually seated in the stern of a real boat.

"This has been a wonderful day!" said he, as the Rat shoved off and took to the sculls again. "Do you know, I've never been in a boat before in all my life."

"What?" cried the Rat, open-mouthed: "Never been in a – you never – well, I – what have you been doing, then?"

"Is it so nice as all that?" asked the Mole shyly, though he was quite prepared to believe it as he leant back in his seat and surveyed the cushions, the oars, the rowlocks, and all the fascinating fittings, and felt the boat sway lightly under him.

"Nice? It's the *only* thing," said the Water Rat solemnly, as he leant forward for his stroke. "Believe me, my young friend, there is *nothing* – absolutely nothing – half so much worth doing as simply messing about in boats. Simply messing," he went on dreamily: "messing – about – in – boats; messing –"

"Look ahead, Rat!" cried the Mole suddenly.

It was too late. The boat struck the bank full tilt. The dreamer, the joyous oarsman, lay on his back at the bottom of the boat, his heels in the air.

"– about in boats – or *with* boats," the Rat went on composedly, picking himself up with a pleasant laugh. "In or out of 'em, it doesn't matter. Nothing seems really to matter, that's the charm of it. Whether you get away, or whether you don't; whether you arrive at your destination or whether you reach somewhere else, or whether you never get anywhere at all, you're always busy, and you never do anything in particular; and when you've done it there's always something else to do, and you can do it if you like, but you'd much better not. Look here! If you've really nothing else on hand this morning, supposing we drop down the river together, and have a long day of it?"

The Mole waggled his toes from sheer happiness, spread his chest with a sigh of full contentment, and leant back blissfully into the soft cushions. "*What* a day I'm having!" he said. "Let us start at once!"

"Hold hard a minute, then!" said the Rat. He looped the painter through a ring in his landing-stage, climbed up into his hole above, and after a short interval reappeared staggering under a fat, wicker luncheon-basket.

"Shove that under your feet," he observed to the Mole, as he passed it down into the boat. Then he untied the painter and took the sculls again.

"What's inside it?" asked the Mole, wriggling with curiosity.

"There's cold chicken inside it," replied the Rat briefly; "coldtonguecoldhamcoldbeef-pickledgherkinssaladfrenchrollscresssandwidgespottedmeatgingerbeerlemonade-sodawater –"

"O stop, stop," cried the Mole in ecstasies: "This is too much!"

"Do you really think so?" inquired the Rat seriously. "It's only what I always take on these little excursions; and the other animals are always telling me that I'm a mean beast and cut it *very* fine!"

The Mole never heard a word he was saying. Absorbed in the new life he was entering upon, intoxicated with the sparkle, the ripple, the scents and the sounds and the sunlight, he trailed a paw in the water and dreamt long waking dreams. The Water Rat, like the good little fellow he was, sculled steadily on and forbore to disturb him.

"I like your clothes awfully, old chap," he remarked after some half hour or so had passed. "I'm going to get a black velvet smoking suit myself some day, as soon as I can afford it."

"I beg your pardon," said the Mole, pulling himself together with an effort. "You must think me very rude; but all this is so new to me. So – this – is – a – River!"

"*The* River," corrected the Rat.

"And you really live by the river? What a jolly life!"

"By it and with it and on it and in it," said the Rat. "It's brother and sister to me, and aunts, and company, and food and drink, and (naturally) washing. It's my world, and I don't want any other. What it hasn't got is not worth having, and what it doesn't know is not worth knowing. Lord! the times we've had together! Whether in winter or summer, spring or autumn, it's always got its fun and its excitements. When the floods are on in February, and my cellars and basement are brimming with drink that's no good to me, and the brown water runs by my best bedroom window; or again when it all drops away and shows patches of mud that smell like plum-cake, and the rushes and weed clog the channels, and I can potter about dry-shod over most of the bed of it and find fresh food to eat, and things careless people have dropped out of boats!"

"But isn't it a bit dull at times?" the Mole ventured to ask. "Just you and the river, and no one else to pass a word with?"

"No one else to – well, I mustn't be hard on you," said the Rat with forbearance. "You're new to it, and of course you don't know. The bank is so crowded nowadays that many people are moving away altogether. O no, it isn't what it used to be, at all. Otters, kingfishers, dabchicks, moorhens, all of them about all day long and always wanting you to *do* something – as if a fellow had no business of his own to attend to!"

"What lies over *there?*" asked the Mole, waving a paw towards a background of woodland that darkly framed the water-meadows on one side of the river.

"That? O, that's just the Wild Wood," said the Rat shortly. "We don't go there very much, we river-bankers."

"Aren't they – aren't they very *nice* people in there?" said the Mole a trifle nervously.

"W-e-ll," replied the Rat, "let me see. The squirrels are all right. *And* the rabbits – some of 'em, but rabbits are a mixed lot. And then there's Badger, of course. He lives right in the heart of it; wouldn't live anywhere else, either, if you paid him to do it. Dear old Badger! Nobody interferes with *him*. They'd better not," he added significantly.

"Why, who *should* interfere with him?" asked the Mole.

"Well, of course – there – are others," explained the Rat in a hesitating sort of way. "Weasels – and stoats – and foxes – and so on. They're all right in a way – I'm very good friends with them – pass the time of day when we meet, and all that – but they break out sometimes, there's no denying it, and then – well, you can't really trust them, and that's the fact."

The Mole knew well that it is quite against animal-etiquette to dwell on possible trouble ahead, or even to allude to it; so he dropped the subject.

"And beyond the Wild Wood again?" he asked: "Where it's all blue and dim, and one sees what may be hills or perhaps they mayn't, and something like the smoke of towns, or is it only cloud-drift?"

"Beyond the Wild Wood comes the Wide World," said the Rat. "And that's something that doesn't matter, either to you or me. I've never been there, and I'm never going, nor you either, if you've got any sense at all. Don't ever refer to it again, please. Now then! Here's our backwater at last, where we're going to lunch."

Leaving the main stream, they now passed into what seemed at first sight like a little land-locked lake. Green turf sloped down to either edge, brown snaky tree-roots gleamed below the surface of the quiet water, while ahead of them the silvery shoulder and foamy tumble of a weir, arm-in-arm with a restless dripping mill-wheel, that held up in its turn a grey-gabled mill-house, filled the air with a soothing murmur of sound, dull and smothery, yet with little clear voices speaking up cheerfully out of it at intervals. It was so very beautiful that the Mole could only hold up both fore-paws and gasp, "O my! O my! O my!"

The Rat brought the boat alongside the bank, made her fast, helped the still awkward Mole safely ashore, and swung out the luncheon-basket. The Mole begged as a favour to be allowed to unpack it all by himself; and the Rat was very pleased to indulge him, and to sprawl at full length on the grass and rest, while his excited friend shook out the table-cloth and spread it, took out all the mysterious packets one by one and arranged their contents in due order, still gasping, "O my! O my!" at each fresh revelation. When all was ready, the Rat said, "Now pitch in, old fellow!" and the Mole was

indeed very glad to obey, for he had started his spring-cleaning at a very early hour that morning, as people *will* do, and had not paused for bite or sup; and he had been through a very great deal since that distant time which now seemed so many days ago.

"What are you looking at?" said the Rat presently, when the edge of their hunger was somewhat dulled, and the Mole's eyes were able to wander off the table-cloth a little.

"I am looking," said the Mole, "at a streak of bubbles that I see travelling along the surface of the water. That is a thing that strikes me as funny."

"Bubbles? Oho!" said the Rat, and chirruped cheerily in an inviting sort of way.

A broad glistening muzzle showed itself above the edge of the bank, and the Otter hauled himself out and shook the water from his coat.

"Greedy beggars!" he observed, making for the provender. "Why didn't you invite me, Ratty?"

"This was an impromptu affair," explained the Rat. "By the way – my friend Mr Mole."

"Proud, I'm sure," said the Otter, and the two animals were friends forthwith.

"Such a rumpus everywhere!" continued the Otter. "All the world seems out on the river to-day. I came up this backwater to try and get a moment's peace, and then stumble upon you fellows! – At least – I beg pardon – I don't exactly mean that, you know."

There was a rustle behind them proceeding from a hedge wherein last year's leaves still clung thick, and a stripy head, with high shoulders behind it, peered forth on them.

"Come on, old Badger!" shouted the Rat.

The Badger trotted forward a pace or two; then grunted, "H'm! Company," and turned his back and disappeared from view.

"That's *just* the sort of fellow he is!" observed the disappointed Rat. "Simply hates Society! Now we shan't see any more of him to-day. Well tell us, *who's* out on the river?"

"Toad's out, for one," replied the Otter. "In his brand-new wager-boat; new togs, new everything!"

The two animals looked at each other and laughed.

"Once, it was nothing but sailing," said the Rat. "Then he tired of that and took to punting. Nothing would please him but to punt all day and every day, and a nice mess he made of it. Last year it was house-boating, and we all had to go and stay with him in his house-boat, and pretend we liked it. He was going to spend the rest of his life in a house-boat. It's all the same, whatever he takes up; he gets tired of it, and starts on something fresh."

"Such a good fellow, too," remarked the Otter reflectively: "But no stability – especially in a boat!"

From where they sat they could get a glimpse of the main stream across the island that separated them; and just then a wager-boat flashed into view, the rower – a short, stout figure – splashing badly and rolling a good deal, but working his hardest. The Rat stood up and hailed him, but Toad – for it was he – shook his head and settled sternly to his work.

"He'll be out of the boat in a minute if he rolls like that," said the Rat, sitting down again.

"Of course he will," chuckled the Otter. "Did I ever tell you that good story about Toad and the lock-keeper? It happened this way. Toad . . ."

An errant May-fly swerved unsteadily athwart the current in the intoxicated fashion affected by young bloods of May-flies seeing life. A swirl of water and a "cloop!" and the May-fly was visible no more.

Neither was the Otter.

The Mole looked down. The voice was still in his ears, but the turf whereon he had sprawled was clearly vacant. Not an otter to be seen, as far as the distant horizon.

But again there was a streak of bubbles on the surface of the river.

The Rat hummed a tune, and the Mole recollected that animal-etiquette forbade any sort of comment on the sudden disappearance of one's friends at any moment, for any reason or no reason whatever.

"Well, well," said the Rat, "I suppose we ought to be moving. I wonder which of us had better pack the luncheon-basket?" He did not speak as if he was frightfully eager for the treat.

"O, please let me," said the Mole. So, of course, the Rat let him.

Packing the basket was not quite such pleasant work as unpacking the basket. It never is. But the Mole was bent on enjoying everything, and although just when he had got the basket packed and strapped up tightly he saw a plate staring up at him from the grass, and when the job had been done again the Rat pointed out a fork which anybody ought to have seen, and last of all, behold! the mustard pot, which he had been sitting on without knowing it – still, somehow, the thing got finished at last, without much loss of temper.

The afternoon sun was getting low as the Rat sculled gently homewards in a dreamy mood, murmuring poetry-things over to himself, and not paying much attention to Mole. But the Mole was very full of lunch, and self-satisfaction, and pride, and already quite at home in a boat (so he thought) and was getting a bit restless besides: and presently he said, "Ratty! Please, *I* want to row, now!"

The Rat shook his head with a smile. "Not yet, my young friend," he said – "wait till you've had a few lessons. It's not so easy as it looks."

The Mole was quiet for a minute or two. But he began to feel more and more jealous of Rat, sculling so strongly and so easily along, and his pride began to whisper that he could do it every bit as well. He jumped up and seized the sculls, so suddenly, that the Rat, who was gazing out over the water and saying more poetry-things to himself, was taken by surprise and fell backwards off his seat with his legs in the air for the second time, while the triumphant Mole took his place and grabbed the sculls with entire confidence.

"Stop it, you *silly* ass!" cried the Rat, from the bottom of the boat. "You can't do it! You'll have us over!"

The Mole flung his sculls back with a flourish, and made a great dig at the water. He missed the surface altogether, his legs flew up above his head, and he found himself lying on the top of the prostrate Rat. Greatly alarmed, he made a grab at the side of the boat, and the next moment – Sploosh!

Over went the boat, and he found himself struggling in the river.

O my, how cold the water was, and O, how *very* wet it felt. How it sang in his ears as he went down, down, down! How bright and welcome the sun looked as he rose to the surface coughing and spluttering! How black was his despair when he felt himself sinking again! Then a firm paw gripped him by the back of his neck. It was the Rat, and he was evidently laughing – the Mole could *feel* him laughing, right down his arm and through his paw, and so into his – the Mole's – neck.

The Rat got hold of a scull and shoved it under the Mole's arm; then he did the same by the other side of him and, swimming behind, propelled the helpless animal to shore, hauled him out, and set him down on the bank, a squashy, pulpy lump of misery.

When the Rat had rubbed him down a bit, and wrung some of the wet out of him, he said, "Now, then, old fellow! Trot up and down the towing-path as hard as you can, till you're warm and dry again, while I dive for the luncheon-basket."

So the dismal Mole, wet without and ashamed within, trotted about till he was fairly dry, while the Rat plunged into the water again, recovered the boat, righted her and made her fast, fetched his floating property to shore by degrees, and finally dived successfully for the luncheon-basket and struggled to land with it.

When all was ready for a start once more, the Mole, limp and dejected, took his seat in the stern of the boat; and as they set off, he said in a low voice, broken with emotion, "Ratty, my generous friend! I am very sorry indeed for my foolish and ungrateful conduct. My heart quite fails me when I think how I might have lost that beautiful luncheon-basket. Indeed, I have been a complete ass, and I know it. Will you overlook it this once and forgive me, and let things go on as before?"

"That's all right, bless you!" responded the Rat cheerily. "What's a little wet to a Water Rat? I'm more in the water than out of it most days. Don't you think any more about it; and, look here! I really think you had better come and stop with me for a little time. It's very plain and rough, you know – not like Toad's house at all – but you haven't seen that yet; still, I can make you comfortable. And I'll teach you to row, and to swim, and you'll soon be as handy on the water as any of us."

The Mole was so touched by his kind manner of speaking that he could find no voice to answer him; and he had to brush away a tear or two with the back of his paw. But the Rat kindly looked in another direction, and presently the Mole's spirits revived again, and he was even able to give some straight back-talk to a couple of moorhens who were sniggering to each other about his bedraggled appearance.

When they got home, the Rat made a bright fire in the parlour, and planted the Mole in an arm-chair in front of it, having fetched down a dressing-gown and slippers for him, and told him river stories till supper-time. Very thrilling stories they were, too, to an earth-dwelling animal like Mole. Stories about weirs, and sudden floods, and leaping pike, and steamers that flung hard bottles

– at least bottles were certainly flung, and *from* steamers, so presumably *by* them; and about herons, and how particular they were whom they spoke to; and about adventures down drains, and night-fishings with Otter, or excursions far afield with Badger. Supper was a most cheerful meal; but very shortly afterwards a terribly sleepy Mole had to be escorted upstairs by his considerate host, to the best bedroom, where he soon laid his head on his pillow in great peace and contentment, knowing that his new-found friend the River was lapping the sill of his window.

This day was only the first of many similar ones for the emancipated Mole, each of them longer and fuller of interest as the ripening summer moved onward. He learnt to swim and to row, and entered into the joy of running water; and with his ear to the reed-stems he caught, at intervals, something of what the wind went whispering so constantly among them.

Chapter 2

The Open Road

"Ratty," said the Mole suddenly, one bright summer morning, "if you please, I want to ask you a favour."

The Rat was sitting on the river bank, singing a little song. He had just composed it himself, so he was very taken up with it, and would not pay proper attention to Mole or anything else. Since early morning he had been swimming in the river in company with his friends the ducks. And when the ducks stood on their heads suddenly, as ducks will, he would dive down and tickle their necks just under where their chins would be if ducks had chins, till they were forced to come to the surface again in a hurry, spluttering and angry and shaking their feathers at him, for it is impossible to say quite *all* you feel when your head is under water. At last they implored him to go away and attend to his own affairs and leave them to mind theirs. So the Rat went away, and sat on the river bank in the sun, and made up a song about them, which he called

"DUCKS' DITTY"

All along the backwater,
Through the rushes tall,
Ducks are a-dabbling,
Up tails all!

Ducks' tails, drakes' tails,
Yellow feet a-quiver,
Yellow bills all out of sight
Busy in the river!

Slushy green undergrowth
Where the roach swim –
Here we keep our larder,
Cool and full and dim.

Everyone for what he likes!
We like to be
Heads down, tails up,
Dabbling free!

High in the blue above
Swifts whirl and call –
We are down a-dabbling
Up tails all!

"I don't know that I think so *very* much of that little song, Rat," observed the Mole cautiously. He was no poet himself and didn't care who knew it; and he had a candid nature.

"Nor don't the ducks neither," replied the Rat cheerfully. "They say, 'Why can't fellows be allowed to do what they like *when* they like and *as* they like, instead of other fellows sitting on banks and watching them all the time and making remarks and poetry and things about them? What *nonsense* it all is!' That's what the ducks say."

"So it is, so it is," said the Mole, with great heartiness.

"No, it isn't!" cried the Rat indignantly.

"Well, then, it isn't, it isn't," replied the Mole soothingly. "But what I wanted to ask you was, won't you take me to call on Mr Toad? I've heard so much about him, and I do so want to make his acquaintance."

"Why, certainly," said the good-natured Rat, jumping to his feet and dismissing poetry from his mind for the day. "Get the boat out, and we'll paddle up there at once. It's never the wrong time to call on Toad. Early or late he's always the same fellow. Always good-tempered, always glad to see you, always sorry when you go!"

"He must be a very nice animal," observed the Mole, as he got into the boat and took the sculls, while the Rat settled himself comfortably in the stern.

"He is indeed the best of animals," replied Rat. "So simple, so good-natured, and so affectionate. Perhaps he's not very clever – we can't all be geniuses; and it may be that he is both boastful and conceited. But he has got some great qualities, has Toady."

Rounding a bend in the river, they came in sight of a handsome, dignified old house of mellowed red brick, with well-kept lawns reaching down to the water's edge.

"There's Toad Hall," said the Rat; "and that creek on the left, where the notice-board says, 'Private. No landing allowed,' leads to his boat-house, where we'll leave the boat. The stables are over there to the right. That's the banqueting-hall you're looking at now – very old, that is. Toad is rather rich, you know, and this is really one of the nicest houses in these parts, though we never admit as much to Toad."

They glided up the creek, and the Mole shipped his sculls as they passed into the shadow of a large boat-house. Here they saw many handsome boats, slung from the cross-beams or hauled up on a slip, but none in the water; and the place had an unused and a deserted air.

The Rat looked around him. "I understand," said he. "Boating is played out. He's tired of it, and done with it. I wonder what new fad he has taken up now? Come along and let's look him up. We shall hear all about it quite soon enough."

They disembarked, and strolled across the gay flower-decked lawns in search of Toad, whom they presently happened upon resting in a wicker garden-chair, with a preoccupied expression of face, and a large map spread out on his knees.

"Hooray!" he cried, jumping up on seeing them, "this is splendid!" He shook the paws of both of them warmly, never waiting for an introduction to the Mole. "How *kind* of you!" he went on, dancing round them. "I was just going to send a boat down the river for you, Ratty, with strict orders that you were to be fetched up here at once, whatever you were doing. I want you badly – both of you. Now what will you take? Come inside and have something! You don't know how lucky it is, your turning up just now!"

"Let's sit quiet a bit, Toady!" said the Rat, throwing himself into an easy chair, while the Mole took another by the side of him and made some civil remark about Toad's "delightful residence".

"Finest house on the whole river," cried Toad boisterously. "Or anywhere else, for that matter," he could not help adding.

Here the Rat nudged the Mole. Unfortunately the Toad saw him do it, and turned very red. There was a moment's painful silence. Then Toad burst out laughing. "All right, Ratty," he said. "It's only my way, you know. And it's not such a very bad house, is it? You know you rather like it yourself. Now, look here. Let's be sensible. You are the very animals I wanted. You've got to help me. It's most important!"

"It's about your rowing, I suppose," said the Rat, with an innocent air. "You're getting on fairly well, though you splash a good bit still. With a great deal of patience, and any quantity of coaching, you may –"

"O, pooh! boating!" interrupted the Toad, in great disgust. "Silly boyish amusement. I've given that up *long* ago. Sheer waste of time, that's what it is. It makes me downright sorry to see you fellows, who ought to know better, spending all your energies in that aimless manner. No, I've discovered the real thing, the only genuine occupation for a lifetime. I propose to devote the remainder of mine to it, and can only regret the wasted years that lie behind me, squandered in trivialities. Come with me, dear Ratty, and your amiable friend also, if he will be so very good, just as far as the stable-yard, and you shall see what you shall see!"

He led the way to the stable-yard accordingly, the Rat following with a most mistrustful expression; and there, drawn out of the coach-house into the open, they saw a gipsy caravan, shining with newness, painted a canary-yellow picked out with green, and red wheels.

"There you are!" cried the Toad, straddling and expanding himself. "There's real life for you, embodied in that little cart. The open road, the dusty highway, the heath, the common, the hedgerows, the rolling downs! Camps, villages, towns, cities! Here to-day, up and off to somewhere else to-morrow! Travel, change, interest, excitement! The whole world before you, and a horizon that's always changing! And mind, this is the finest cart of its sort that was ever built, without any exception. Come inside and look at the arrangements. Planned 'em all myself, I did!"

The Mole was tremendously interested and excited, and followed him eagerly up the steps and into the interior of the caravan. The Rat only snorted and thrust his hands deep into his pockets, remaining where he was.

It was indeed very compact and comfortable. Little sleeping-bunks – a little table that folded up against the wall – a cooking stove, lockers, bookshelves, a bird-cage with a bird in it; and pots, pans, jugs and kettles of every size and variety.

"All complete!" said the Toad triumphantly, pulling open a locker. "You see – biscuits, potted lobster, sardines – everything you can possibly want. Soda-water here – baccy there – letter-paper, bacon, jam, cards and dominoes – you'll find," he continued, as they descended the steps again, "you'll find that nothing whatever has been forgotten, when we make our start this afternoon."

"I beg your pardon," said the Rat slowly, as he chewed a straw, "but did I overhear you say something about '*we*', and '*start*', and '*this afternoon*'?"

"Now, you dear good old Ratty," said Toad imploringly, "don't begin talking in that stiff and sniffy sort of way, because you know you've *got* to come. I can't possibly manage without you, so please consider it settled, and don't argue – it's the one thing I can't stand. You surely don't mean to stick to your dull fusty old river all your life, and just live in a hole in a bank, and *boat*? I want to show you the world! I'm going to make an *animal* of you, my boy!"

"I don't care," said the Rat doggedly. "I'm not coming, and that's flat. And I *am* going to stick to my old river, *and* live in a hole, *and* boat, as I've always done. And what's more, Mole's going to stick to me and do as I do, aren't you, Mole?"

"Of course I am," said the Mole loyally. "I'll always stick to you, Rat, and what you say is to be – has got to be. All the same, it sounds as if it might have been – well, rather fun, you know!" he added wistfully. Poor Mole! The Life Adventurous was so new a thing to him, and so thrilling; and this fresh aspect of it was so tempting; and he had fallen in love at first sight with the canary-coloured cart and all its little fitments.

The Rat saw what was passing in his mind, and wavered. He hated disappointing people, and he was fond of the Mole, and would do almost anything to oblige him. Toad was watching both of them closely.

"Come along in and have some lunch," he said diplomatically, "and we'll talk it over. We needn't decide anything in a hurry. Of course, *I* don't really care. I only want to give pleasure to you fellows. 'Live for others!' That's my motto in life."

During luncheon – which was excellent, of course, as everything at Toad Hall always was – the Toad simply let himself go. Disregarding the Rat, he proceeded to play upon the inexperienced Mole as on a harp. Naturally a voluble animal, and always mastered by his imagination, he painted the prospects of the trip and the joys of the open life and the roadside in such glowing colours that the Mole could hardly sit in his chair for excitement. Somehow, it soon seemed taken for granted by all three of them that the trip was a settled thing; and the Rat, though still unconvinced in his mind, allowed his good-nature to override his personal objections. He could not bear to disappoint his two friends, who were already deep in schemes and anticipations, planning out each day's separate occupation for several weeks ahead.

When they were quite ready, the now triumphant Toad led his companions to the paddock and set them to capture the old grey horse, who, without having been consulted, and to his own extreme annoyance, had been told off by Toad for the dustiest job in this dusty expedition. He frankly preferred the paddock, and took a deal of catching. Meantime Toad packed the lockers still tighter with

necessaries, and hung nose-bags, nets of onions, bundles of hay, and baskets from the bottom of the cart. At last the horse was caught and harnessed, and they set off, all talking at once, each animal either trudging by the side of the cart or sitting on the shaft, as the humour took him. It was a golden afternoon. The smell of the dust they kicked up was rich and satisfying; out of thick orchards on either side the road, birds called and whistled to them cheerily; good-natured wayfarers, passing them, gave them "Good day," or stopped to say nice things about their beautiful cart; and rabbits, sitting at their front doors in the hedgerows, held up their fore-paws, and said, "O my! O my! O my!"

Late in the evening, tired and happy and miles from home, they drew up on a remote common far from habitations, turned the horse loose to graze, and ate their simple supper sitting on the grass by the side of the cart. Toad talked big about all he was going to do in the days to come, while stars grew fuller and larger all around them, and a yellow moon, appearing suddenly and silently from nowhere in particular, came to keep them company and listen to their talk. At last they turned into their little bunks in the cart; and Toad, kicking out his legs, sleepily said, "Well, good night, you fellows! This is the real life for a gentleman! Talk about your old river!"

"I *don't* talk about my river," replied the patient Rat. "You *know* I don't, Toad. But I *think* about it," he added pathetically, in a lower tone: "I think about it – all the time!"

The Mole reached out from under his blanket, felt for the Rat's paw in the darkness, and gave it a squeeze. "I'll do whatever you like, Ratty," he whispered. "Shall we run away to-morrow morning, quite early – *very* early – and go back to our dear old hole on the river?"

"No, no, we'll see it out," whispered back the Rat. "Thanks awfully, but I ought to stick by Toad till this trip is ended. It wouldn't be safe for him to be left to himself. It won't take very long. His fads never do. Good night!"

The end was indeed nearer than even the Rat suspected.

After so much open air and excitement the Toad slept very soundly, and no amount of shaking could rouse him out of bed next morning. So the Mole and Rat turned to, quietly and manfully, and while the Rat saw to the horse, and lit a fire, and cleaned last night's cups and platters, and got things ready for breakfast, the Mole trudged off to the nearest village, a long way off, for milk and eggs and various necessaries the Toad had, of course, forgotten to provide. The hard work had all been done, and the two animals were resting, thoroughly exhausted, by the time Toad appeared on the scene, fresh and gay, remarking what a pleasant easy life it was they were all leading now, after the cares and worries and fatigues of housekeeping at home.

They had a pleasant ramble that day over grassy downs and along narrow by-lanes, and camped, as before, on a common, only this time the two guests took care that Toad should do his fair share of work. In consequence, when the time came for starting next morning, Toad was by no means so rapturous about the simplicity of the primitive life, and indeed attempted to resume his place in his bunk, whence he was hauled by force. Their way lay, as before, across country by narrow lanes, and it was not till the afternoon that

they came out on the high road, their first high road; and there disaster, fleet and unforeseen, sprang out on them – disaster momentous indeed to their expedition, but simply overwhelming in its effect on the after-career of Toad.

They were strolling along the high road easily, the Mole by the horse's head, talking to him, since the horse had complained that he was being frightfully left out of it, and nobody considered him in the least; the Toad and the Water Rat walking behind the cart talking together – at least Toad was talking, and Rat was saying at intervals, "Yes, precisely; and what did *you* say to *him?*"– and thinking all the time of something very different, when far behind them they heard a faint warning hum, like the drone of a distant bee. Glancing back, they saw a small cloud of dust, with a dark centre of energy, advancing on

them at incredible speed, while from out the dust a faint "Poop-poop!" wailed like an uneasy animal in pain. Hardly regarding it, they turned to resume their conversation, when in an instant (as it seemed) the peaceful scene was changed, and with a blast of wind

and a whirl of sound that made them jump for the nearest ditch, it was on them! The "poop-poop" rang with a brazen shout in their ears, they had a moment's glimpse of an interior of glittering plate-glass and rich morocco, and the magnificent motor-car, immense, breath-snatching, passionate, with its pilot tense and hugging his wheel, possessed all earth and air for the fraction of a second, flung an enveloping cloud of dust that blinded and enwrapped them utterly, and then dwindled to a speck in the far distance, changed back into a droning bee once more.

The old grey horse, dreaming, as he plodded along, of his quiet paddock, in a new raw situation such as this simply abandoned himself to his natural emotions. Rearing, plunging, backing steadily, in spite of all the Mole's efforts at his head, and all the Mole's lively language directed at his better feelings, he drove the cart backwards towards the deep ditch at the side of the road. It wavered an instant – then there was a heart-rending crash – and the canary-coloured cart, their pride and their joy, lay on its side in the ditch, an irredeemable wreck.

The Rat danced up and down in the road, simply transported with passion. "You villains!" he shouted, shaking both fists. "You scoundrels, you highwaymen, you – you – road-hogs! – I'll have the law on you! I'll report you! I'll take you through all the Courts!" His home-sickness had quite slipped away from him, and for the moment he was the skipper of the canary-coloured vessel driven on a shoal by the reckless jockeying of rival mariners, and he was trying to recollect all the fine and biting things he used to say to masters of steam-launches when their wash, as they drove too near the bank, used to flood his parlour carpet at home.

Toad sat straight down in the middle of the dusty road, his legs stretched out before him, and stared fixedly in the direction of the disappearing motor-car. He breathed short, his face wore a placid, satisfied expression, and at intervals he faintly murmured "Poop-poop!"

The Mole was busy trying to quiet the horse, which he succeeded in doing after a time. Then he went to look at the cart, on its side in the ditch. It was indeed a sorry sight. Panels and windows smashed, axles hopelessly bent, one wheel off, sardine-tins scattered over the wide world, and the bird in the bird-cage sobbing pitifully and calling to be let out.

The Rat came to help him, but their united efforts were not sufficient to right the cart. "Hi! Toad!" they cried. "Come and bear a hand, can't you!"

The Toad never answered a word, or budged from his seat in the road; so they went to see what was the matter with him. They found him in a sort of trance, a happy smile on his face, his eyes still fixed on the dusty wake of their destroyer. At intervals he was still heard to murmur "Poop-poop!"

The Rat shook him by the shoulder. "Are you coming to help us, Toad?" he demanded sternly.

"Glorious, stirring sight!" murmured Toad, never offering to move. "The poetry of motion! The *real* way to travel! The *only* way to travel! Here to-day – in next week to-morrow! Villages skipped, towns and cities jumped – always somebody else's horizon! O bliss! O poop-poop! O my! O my!"

"O *stop* being an ass, Toad!" cried the Mole despairingly.

"And to think I never *knew*!" went on the Toad in a dreamy monotone. "All those wasted years that lie behind me, I never knew, never even *dreamt*! But *now* – but now that I know, now that I fully realize! O what a flowery track lies spread before me, henceforth! What dust-clouds shall spring up behind me as I speed on my reckless way! What carts I shall fling carelessly into the ditch in the wake of my magnificent onset! Horrid little carts – common carts – canary-coloured carts!"

"What are we to do with him?" asked the Mole of the Water Rat.

"Nothing at all," replied the Rat firmly. "Because there is really nothing to be done. You see, I know him from of old. He is now possessed. He has got a new craze, and it always takes him that way, in its first stage. He'll continue like that for days now, like an animal walking in a happy dream, quite useless for all practical purposes. Never mind him. Let's go and see what there is to be done about the cart."

A careful inspection showed them that, even if they succeeded in righting it by themselves, the cart would travel no longer. The axles were in a hopeless state, and the missing wheel was shattered into pieces.

The Rat knotted the horse's reins over his back and took him by the head, carrying the bird-cage and its hysterical occupant in the other hand. "Come on!" he said grimly to the Mole. "It's five or six miles to the nearest town, and we shall just have to walk it. The sooner we make a start the better."

"But what about Toad?" asked the Mole anxiously, as they set off together. "We can't leave him here, sitting in the middle of the road by himself, in the distracted state he's in! It's not safe. Supposing another Thing were to come along?"

"O, *bother* Toad," said the Rat savagely; "I've done with him!"

They had not proceeded very far on their way, however, when there was a pattering of feet behind them, and Toad caught them up and thrust a paw inside the elbow of each of them; still breathing short and staring into vacancy.

"Now, look here, Toad!" said the Rat sharply: "as soon as we get to the town, you'll have to go straight to the police-station, and see if they know anything about that motor-car and who it belongs to, and lodge a complaint against it. And then you'll have to go to a blacksmith's or a wheelwright's and arrange for the cart to be fetched and mended and put to rights. It'll take time, but it's not quite a hopeless smash. Meanwhile, the Mole and I will go to an inn and find comfortable rooms where we can stay till the cart's ready, and till your nerves have recovered their shock."

"Police-station! Complaint!" murmured Toad dreamily. "Me *complain* of that beautiful, that heavenly vision that has been vouchsafed me! *Mend* the *cart*! I've done with carts for ever. I never want to see the cart, or to hear of it, again. O, Ratty! You can't think how obliged I am to you for consenting to come on this trip! I wouldn't have gone without you, and then I might never have seen that – that swan, that sunbeam, that thunderbolt! I might never have heard that entrancing sound, or smelt that bewitching smell! I owe it all to you, my best of friends!"

The Rat turned from him in despair. "You see what it is?" he said to the Mole, addressing him across Toad's head: "He's quite hopeless. I give it up – when we get to the town we'll go to the railway-station, and with luck we may pick up a train there that'll get us back to river bank to-night. And if ever

you catch me going a-pleasuring with this provoking animal again!" –
He snorted, and during the rest of that weary trudge addressed his remarks
exclusively to Mole.

On reaching the town they went straight to the station and deposited Toad
in the second-class waiting-room, giving a porter twopence to keep a strict eye
on him. They then left the horse at an inn stable, and gave what directions they
could about the cart and its contents. Eventually, a slow train having landed
them at a station not very far from Toad Hall, they escorted the spell-bound,
sleep-walking Toad to his door, put him inside it, and instructed his housekeeper
to feed him, undress him, and put him to bed. Then they got out their boat
from the boat-house, sculled down the river home, and at a very late hour sat
down to supper in their own cosy river-side parlour, to the Rat's great joy and
contentment.

The following evening the Mole, who had risen late and taken things
very easy all day, was sitting on the bank fishing, when the Rat, who had been
looking up his friends and gossiping, came strolling along to find him. "Heard
the news?" he said. "There's nothing else being talked about, all along the river
bank. Toad went up to Town by an early train this morning. And he has ordered
a large and very expensive motor-car."

Chapter 3

The Wild Wood

The Mole had long wanted to make the acquaintance of the Badger. He seemed, by all accounts, to be such an important personage and, though rarely visible, to make his unseen influence felt by everybody about the place. But whenever the Mole mentioned his wish to the Water Rat he always found himself put off. "It's all right," the Rat would say. "Badger'll turn up some day or other – he's always turning up – and then I'll introduce you. The best of fellows! But you must not only take him *as* you find him, but *when* you find him."

"Couldn't you ask him here – dinner or something?" said the Mole.

"He wouldn't come," replied the Rat simply. "Badger hates Society, and invitations, and dinner, and all that sort of thing."

"Well, then, supposing we go and call on *him?*" suggested the Mole.

"O, I'm sure he wouldn't like that at *all*," said the Rat, quite alarmed. "He's so very shy, he'd be sure to be offended. I've never even ventured to call on him at his own home myself, though I know him so well. Besides, we can't. It's quite out of the question, because he lives in the very middle of the Wild Wood."

"Well, supposing he does," said the Mole. "You told me the Wild Wood was all right, you know."

"O, I know, I know, so it is," replied the Rat evasively. "But I think we won't go there just now. Not *just* yet. It's a long way, and he wouldn't be at home at this time of year anyhow, and he'll be coming along some day, if you'll wait quietly."

The Mole had to be content with this. But the Badger never came along, and every day brought its amusements, and it was not till summer was long over, and cold and frost and miry ways kept them much indoors, and the swollen river raced past outside their windows with a speed that mocked at boating of any sort or kind, that he found his thoughts dwelling again with much persistence on the solitary grey Badger, who lived his own life by himself, in his hole in the middle of the Wild Wood.

In the winter time the Rat slept a great deal, retiring early and rising late. During his short day he sometimes scribbled poetry or did other small domestic jobs about the house; and, of course there were always animals dropping in for a chat, and consequently there was a good deal of story-telling and comparing notes on the past summer and all its doings.

Such a rich chapter it had been, when one came to look back on it all! With illustrations so numerous and so very highly coloured! The pageant of the river bank had marched steadily along, unfolding itself in scene-pictures that succeeded each other in stately procession. Purple loose-strife arrived early, shaking luxuriant tangled locks along the edge of the mirror whence its own face laughed back at it. Willow-herb, tender and wistful, like a pink sunset cloud, was not slow to follow. Comfrey, the purple hand-in-hand with the white, crept forth to take its place in the line; and at last one morning the diffident and delaying dog-rose stepped delicately on the stage, and one knew, as if string-music had announced it in stately chords that strayed into a gavotte, that June at last was here. One member of the company was still awaited; the shepherd-boy for the nymphs to woo, the knight for whom the ladies waited at the window, the prince that was to kiss the sleeping summer back to life and love. But when meadow-sweet, debonair and odorous in amber jerkin, moved graciously to his place in the group, then the play was ready to begin.

And what a play it had been! Drowsy animals, snug in their holes while wind and rain were battering at their doors, recalled still keen mornings, an hour before sunrise, when the white mist, as yet undispersed, clung closely along the surface of the water; then the shock of the early plunge, the scamper along the bank, and the radiant transformation of earth, air, and water, when suddenly the sun was with them again, and grey was gold and colour was born and sprang out of the earth once more. They recalled the languorous siesta of hot midday, deep in green undergrowth, the sun striking through in tiny golden shafts and spots; the boating and bathing of the afternoon, the rambles along dusty lanes and through yellow cornfields; and the long, cool evening at last, when so many threads were gathered up, so many friendships rounded, and so many adventures planned for the morrow. There was plenty to talk about on those short winter days when the animals found themselves round the fire; still, the Mole had a good deal of spare time on his hands, and so one afternoon, when the Rat in his arm-chair before the blaze was alternately dozing and trying over rhymes that wouldn't fit, he formed the resolution to go out by himself and explore the Wild Wood, and perhaps strike up an acquaintance with Mr Badger.

It was a cold still afternoon with a hard steely sky overhead, when he slipped out of the warm parlour into the open air. The country lay bare and entirely leafless around him, and he thought that he had never seen so far and so intimately into the inside of things as on that winter day when Nature was deep in her annual slumber and seemed to have kicked the clothes off. Copses, dells, quarries and all hidden places, which had been mysterious mines for exploration in leafy summer, now exposed themselves and their secrets pathetically, and seemed to ask him to overlook their shabby poverty for a while, till they could riot in rich masquerade as before, and trick and entice him with the old deceptions. It was pitiful in a way, and yet cheering – even exhilarating. He was glad that he liked the country undecorated, hard, and stripped of its finery. He had got down to the bare bones of it, and they were fine and strong and simple. He did not want the warm clover and the play of seeding grasses; the screens of quickset, the billowy drapery of beech and elm seemed best away; and with great cheerfulness of spirit he pushed on towards the Wild Wood, which lay before him low and threatening, like a black reef in some still southern sea.

There was nothing to alarm him at first entry. Twigs crackled under his feet, logs tripped him, funguses on stumps resembled caricatures, and startled him for the moment by their likeness to something familiar and far away; but that was all fun, and exciting. It led him on, and he penetrated to where the light was less, and trees crouched nearer and nearer, and holes made ugly mouths at him on either side.

Everything was very still now. The dusk advanced on him steadily, rapidly, gathering in behind and before; and the light seemed to be draining away like flood-water.

Then the faces began.

It was over his shoulder, and indistinctly, that he first thought he saw a face: a little evil wedge-shaped face, looking out at him from a hole. When he turned and confronted it, the thing had vanished.

He quickened his pace, telling himself cheerfully not to begin imagining things, or there would be simply no end to it. He passed another hole, and another, and another; and then – yes! – no! – yes! certainly a little narrow face, with hard eyes, had flashed up for an instant from a hole, and was gone. He

hesitated – braced himself up for an effort and strode on. Then suddenly, as if it had been so all the time, every hole, far and near, and there were hundreds of them, seemed to possess its face, coming and going rapidly, all fixing on him glances of malice and hatred: all hard-eyed and evil and sharp.

If he could only get away from the holes in the banks, he thought, there would be no more faces. He swung off the path and plunged into the untrodden places of the wood.

Then the whistling began.

Very faint and shrill it was, and far behind him, when first he heard it; but somehow it made him hurry forward. Then, still very faint and shrill, it sounded far ahead of him, and made him hesitate and want to go back. As he halted in indecision it broke out on either side, and seemed to be caught up and passed on throughout the whole length of the wood to its farthest limit. They were up and alert and ready, evidently, whoever they were! And he – he was alone, and unarmed, and far from any help; and the night was closing in.

Then the pattering began.

He thought it was only falling leaves at first, so slight and delicate was the sound of it. Then as it grew it took a regular rhythm, and he knew it for nothing else but the pat-pat-pat of little feet, still a very long way off. Was it in front or behind? It seemed to be first one, then the other, then both. It grew and it multiplied, till from every quarter as he listened anxiously, leaning this way and that, it seemed to be closing in on him. As he stood still to hearken, a rabbit came running hard towards him through the trees. He waited, expecting it to slacken pace, or to swerve from him into a different course. Instead, the animal almost brushed him as it dashed past, his face set and hard, his eyes staring. "Get out of this, you fool, get out!" the Mole heard him mutter as he swung round a stump and disappeared down a friendly burrow.

The pattering increased till it sounded like sudden hail on the dry-leaf carpet spread around him. The whole wood seemed running now, running hard, hunting, chasing, closing in round something or – somebody? In panic, he began to run too, aimlessly, he knew not whither. He ran up against things, he fell over things and into things, he darted under things and dodged round things. At last he took refuge in the deep dark hollow of an old beech tree, which offered shelter, concealment – perhaps even safety, but who could tell? Anyhow, he was too tired to run any further, and could only snuggle down into the dry leaves which had drifted into the hollow and hope he was safe for the time. And as he lay there panting and trembling, and listened to the whistlings and the patterings outside, he knew it at last, in all its fullness, that dread thing which other little dwellers in field and hedgerow had encountered here, and known as their darkest moment – that thing, which the Rat had vainly tried to shield him from – the Terror of the Wild Wood!

Meantime the Rat, warm and comfortable, dozed by his fireside. His paper of half-finished verses slipped from his knee, his head fell back, his mouth opened, and he wandered by the verdant banks of dream-rivers. Then a coal slipped, the fire crackled and sent up a spurt of flame, and

he woke with a start. Remembering what he had been engaged upon, he reached down to the floor for his verses, pored over them for a minute, and then looked round for the Mole to ask him if he knew a good rhyme for something or other.

But the Mole was not there.

He listened for a time. The house seemed very quiet.

Then he called "Moly!" several times,

and, receiving no answer, got up and went out into the hall.

The Mole's cap was missing from its accustomed peg. His goloshes, which always lay by the umbrella-stand, were also gone.

The Rat left the house and carefully examined the muddy surface of the ground outside, hoping to find the Mole's tracks. There they were, sure enough. The goloshes were new, just bought for the winter, and the pimples on their soles were fresh and sharp. He could see the imprints of them in the mud, running along straight and purposeful, leading direct to the Wild Wood.

The Rat looked very grave, and stood in deep thought for a minute or two. Then he re-entered the house, strapped a belt round his waist, shoved a brace of pistols into it, took up a stout cudgel that stood in a corner of the hall, and set off for the Wild Wood at a smart pace.

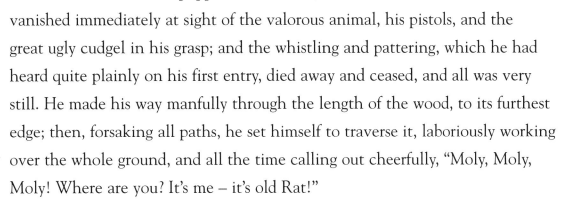

It was already getting towards dusk when he reached the first fringe of trees and plunged without hesitation into the wood, looking anxiously on either side for any sign of his friend. Here and there wicked little faces popped out of holes, but vanished immediately at sight of the valorous animal, his pistols, and the great ugly cudgel in his grasp; and the whistling and pattering, which he had heard quite plainly on his first entry, died away and ceased, and all was very still. He made his way manfully through the length of the wood, to its furthest edge; then, forsaking all paths, he set himself to traverse it, laboriously working over the whole ground, and all the time calling out cheerfully, "Moly, Moly, Moly! Where are you? It's me – it's old Rat!"

He had patiently hunted through the wood for an hour or more, when at last to his joy he heard a little answering cry. Guiding himself by the sound, he made his way through the gathering darkness to the foot of an old beech tree, with a hole in it, and from out of the hole came a feeble voice, saying, "Ratty! Is that really you?"

The Rat crept into the hollow, and there he found the Mole, exhausted and still trembling. "O Rat!" he cried, "I've been so frightened, you can't think!"

"O, I quite understand," said the Rat soothingly. "You shouldn't really have gone and done it, Mole. I did my best to keep you from it. We river-bankers, we hardly ever come here by ourselves. If we have to come, we come in couples, at least; then we're generally all right. Besides, there are a hundred things one has to know, which we understand all about and you don't, as yet. I mean pass-words, and signs, and sayings which have power and effect, and plants you carry in your pocket, and verses you repeat, and dodges and tricks you practise; all simple enough when you know them, but they've got to be known if you're small, or you'll find yourself in trouble. Of course if you were Badger or Otter, it would be quite another matter."

"Surely the brave Mr Toad wouldn't mind coming here by himself, would he?" inquired the Mole.

"Old Toad?" said the Rat, laughing heartily. "He wouldn't show his face here alone, not for a whole hatful of golden guineas, Toad wouldn't."

The Mole was greatly cheered by the sound of the Rat's careless laughter, as well as by the sight of his stick and his gleaming pistols, and he stopped shivering and began to feel bolder and more himself again.

"Now then," said the Rat presently, "we really must pull ourselves together and make a start for home while there's still a little light left. It will never do to spend the night here, you understand. Too cold for one thing."

"Dear Ratty," said the poor Mole, "I'm dreadfully sorry, but I'm simply dead beat and that's a solid fact. You *must* let me rest here a while longer, and get my strength back, if I'm to get home at all."

"O, all right," said the good-natured Rat, "rest away. It's pretty nearly pitch dark now, anyhow, and there ought to be a bit of moon later."

So the Mole got well into the dry leaves and stretched himself out, and presently dropped off into sleep, though of a broken and troubled sort; while the Rat covered himself up, too, as best he might, for warmth, and lay patiently waiting, with a pistol in his paw.

When at last the Mole woke up, much refreshed and in his usual spirits, the Rat said, "Now then! I'll just take a look outside and see if everything's quiet, and then we really must be off."

He went to the entrance of their retreat and put his head out.

Then the Mole heard him saying quietly to himself, "Hullo! hullo! here – *is* – a – go!"

"What's up, Ratty?" asked the Mole.

"*Snow* is up," replied the Rat briefly; "or rather, *down*. It's snowing hard."

The Mole came and crouched beside him, and, looking out, saw the wood that had been so dreadful to him in quite a changed aspect. Holes, hollows, pools, pitfalls, and other black menaces to the wayfarer were vanishing fast, and a gleaming carpet of faery was springing up everywhere, that looked too delicate to be trodden upon by rough feet. A fine powder filled the air and caressed the cheek with a tingle in its touch, and the black boles of the trees showed up in a light that seemed to come from below.

"Well, well, it can't be helped," said the Rat, after pondering. "We must make a start, and take our chance, I suppose. The worst of it is, I don't know exactly where we are. And now this snow makes everything look so very different."

It did indeed. The Mole would not have known that it was the same wood. However, they set out bravely, and took the line that seemed most promising, holding on to each other and pretending with invincible cheerfulness that they recognized an old friend in every fresh tree that grimly and silently greeted them, or saw openings, gaps, or paths with a familiar turn in them, in the monotony of white space and black tree-trunks that refused to vary.

An hour or two later – they had lost all count of time – they pulled up, dispirited, weary, and hopelessly at sea, and sat down on a fallen tree-trunk to recover their breath and consider what was to be done. They were aching with fatigue and bruised with tumbles; they had fallen into several holes and got wet through; the snow was getting so deep that they could hardly drag their little legs through it, and the trees were thicker and more like each other than ever. There seemed to be no end to this wood, and no beginning, and no difference in it, and worst of all, no way out.

"We can't sit here very long," said the Rat. "We shall have to make another push for it, and do something or other. The cold is too awful for anything, and the snow will soon be too deep for us to wade through." He peered about him and considered. "Look here," he went on, "this is what occurs to me. There's a sort of dell down there in front of us, where the ground seems all hilly and humpy and hummocky. We'll make our way down into that, and try and find some sort of shelter, a cave or hole with a dry floor to it, out of the snow and the wind, and there we'll have a good rest before we try again, for we're both of us pretty dead beat. Besides, the snow may leave off, or something may turn up."

So once more they got on their feet, and struggled down into the dell, where they hunted about for a cave or some corner that was dry and a protection from the keen wind and the whirling snow. They were investigating one of the hummocky bits the Rat had spoken of, when suddenly the Mole tripped up and fell forward on his face with a squeal.

"O, my leg!" he cried. "O my poor shin!" and he sat up on the snow and nursed his leg in both his front paws.

"Poor old Mole!" said the Rat kindly. "You don't seem to be having much luck to-day, do you? Let's have a look at the leg. Yes," he went on, going down on his knees to look, "you've cut your shin, sure enough. Wait till I get at my handkerchief, and I'll tie it up for you."

"I must have tripped over a hidden branch or a stump," said the Mole miserably. "O my! O my!"

"It's a very clean cut," said the Rat, examining it again attentively. "That was never done by a branch or a stump. Looks as if it was made by a sharp edge of something in metal. Funny!" He pondered awhile, and examined the humps and slopes that surrounded them.

"Well, never mind what done it," said the Mole, forgetting his grammar in his pain. "It hurts just the same, whatever done it."

But the Rat, after carefully tying up the leg with his handkerchief, had left him and was busy scraping in the snow. He scratched and shovelled and explored, all four legs working busily, while the Mole waited impatiently, remarking at intervals, "O, *come* on, Rat!"

Suddenly the Rat cried "Hooray!" and then "Hooray-oo-ray-oo-ray-oo-ray!" and fell to executing a feeble jig in the snow.

"What *have* you found, Ratty?" asked the Mole, still nursing his leg.

"Come and see!" said the delighted Rat, as he jigged on.

The Mole hobbled up to the spot and had a good look.

"Well," he said at last, slowly, "I *see* it right enough. Seen the same sort of thing before, lots of times. Familiar object, I call it. A door-scraper! Well, what of it? Why dance jigs round a door-scraper?"

"But don't you see what it *means*, you – you dull-witted animal?" cried the Rat impatiently.

"Of course I see what it means," replied the Mole. "It simply means that some *very* careless and forgetful person has left his door-scraper lying about in the middle of the Wild Wood, *just* where it's *sure* to trip *everybody* up. Very thoughtless of him, I call it. When I get home I shall go and complain about it to – to somebody or other, see if I don't!"

"O dear! O dear!" cried the Rat, in despair at his obtuseness. "Here, stop arguing and come and scrape!" And he set to work again and made the snow fly in all directions around him.

After some further toil his efforts were rewarded, and a very shabby door-mat lay exposed to view.

"There, what did I tell you?" exclaimed the Rat in great triumph.

"Absolutely nothing whatever," replied the Mole, with perfect truthfulness. "Well now," he went on, "you seem to have found another piece of domestic litter, done for and thrown away, and I suppose you're perfectly happy. Better go ahead and dance your jig round that if you've got to, and get it over, and then perhaps we can go on and not waste any more time over rubbish-heaps. Can we *eat* a door-mat? Or sleep under a door-mat? Or sit on a door-mat and sledge home over the snow on it, you exasperating rodent?"

"Do – you – mean – to – say," cried the excited Rat, "that this door-mat doesn't *tell* you anything?"

"Really, Rat," said the Mole quite pettishly, "I think we've had enough of this folly. Who ever heard of a door-mat *telling* anyone anything? They simply don't do it. They are not that sort at all. Door-mats know their place."

"Now look here, you – you thick-headed beast," replied the Rat, really angry, "this must stop. Not another word, but scrape – scrape and scratch and dig and hunt round, especially on the sides of the hummocks, if you want to sleep dry and warm to-night, for it's our last chance!"

The Rat attacked a snow-bank beside them with ardour, probing with his cudgel everywhere and then digging with fury; and the Mole scraped busily too, more to oblige the Rat than for any other reason, for his opinion was that his friend was getting light-headed.

Some ten minutes' hard work, and the point of the Rat's cudgel struck something that sounded hollow. He worked till he could get a paw through and feel; then called the Mole to come and help him. Hard at it went the two animals, till at last the result of their labours stood full in view of the astonished and hitherto incredulous Mole.

In the side of what had seemed to be a snow-bank stood a solid-looking little door, painted a dark green. An iron bell-pull hung by the side, and below it, on a small brass plate, neatly engraved in square capital letters, they could read by the aid of moonlight:

MR BADGER

The Mole fell backwards on the snow from sheer surprise and delight. "Rat!" he cried in penitence, "you're a wonder! A real wonder, that's what you are. I see it all now! You argued it out, step by step, in that wise head of yours, from the very moment that I fell and cut my shin, and you looked at the cut, and at once your majestic mind said to itself, 'Door-scraper!' And then you turned to and found the very door-scraper that done it! Did you stop there? No. Some people would have been quite satisfied; but not you. Your intellect went on working. 'Let me only just find a door-mat,' says you to yourself, 'and my theory is proved!' And of course you found your door-mat. You're so clever, I believe you could find anything you liked. 'Now,' says you, 'that door exists, as plain as if I saw it. There's nothing else remains to be done but to find it!' Well, I've read about that sort of thing in books, but I've never come across it before in real life. You ought to go where you'll be properly appreciated. You're simply wasted here, among us fellows. If I only had your head, Ratty –"

"But as you haven't," interrupted the Rat rather unkindly, "I suppose you're going to sit on the snow all night and *talk*? Get up at once and hang on to that bell-pull you see there, and ring hard, as hard as you can, while I hammer!"

While the Rat attacked the door with his stick, the Mole sprang up at the bell-pull, clutched it and swung there, both his feet well off the ground, and from quite a long way off they could faintly hear a deep-toned bell respond.

Chapter 4

Mr Badger

They waited patiently for what seemed a very long time, stamping in the snow to keep their feet warm. At last they heard the sound of slow shuffling footsteps approaching the door from the inside. It seemed, as the Mole remarked to the Rat, like someone walking in carpet slippers that were too large for him and down at heel; which was intelligent of Mole, because that was exactly what it was.

There was the noise of a bolt shot back, and the door opened a few inches, enough to show a long snout and a pair of sleepy blinking eyes.

"Now, the *very* next time this happens," said a gruff and suspicious voice, "I shall be exceedingly angry. Who is it *this* time, disturbing people on such a night? Speak up!"

"O, Badger," cried the Rat, "let us in, please. It's me, Rat, and my friend Mole, and we've lost our way in the snow."

"What, Ratty, my dear little man!" exclaimed the Badger, in quite a different voice. "Come along in, both of you, at once. Why, you must be perished. Well I never! Lost in the snow! And in the Wild Wood, too, and at this time of night! But come in with you."

The two animals tumbled over each other in their eagerness to get inside, and heard the door shut behind them with great joy and relief.

The Badger, who wore a long dressing-gown, and whose slippers were indeed very down-at-heel, carried a flat candlestick in his paw and had probably been on his way to bed when their summons sounded. He looked kindly down on them and patted both their heads. "This is not the sort of night for small animals to be out," he said paternally. "I'm afraid you've been up to some of your pranks again, Ratty. But come along; come into the kitchen. There's a first-rate fire there, and supper and everything."

He shuffled on in front of them, carrying the light, and they followed him, nudging each other in an anticipating sort of way, down a long, gloomy, and, to tell the truth, decidedly shabby passage, into a sort of a central hall, out of which they could dimly see other long tunnel-like passages branching, passages

mysterious and without apparent end. But there were doors in the hall as well –
stout oaken comfortable-looking doors. One of these the Badger flung open, and
at once they found themselves in all the glow and warmth of a large fire-lit
kitchen.

The floor was well-worn red brick, and on the wide hearth burnt a fire of
logs, between two attractive chimney-corners tucked away in the wall, well out
of any suspicion of draught. A couple of high-backed settles, facing each other
on either side of the fire, gave further sitting accommodation for the sociably
disposed. In the middle of the room stood a long table of plain boards placed on
trestles, with benches down each side. At one end of it, where an arm-chair
stood pushed back, were spread the remains of the Badger's plain but ample
supper. Rows of spotless plates winked from the shelves of the dresser at the far
end of the room, and from the rafters overhead hung hams, bundles of dried
herbs, nets of onions, and baskets of eggs. It seemed a place where heroes
could fitly feast after victory, where weary harvesters could line up in scores
along the table and keep their Harvest Home with mirth and song, or where
two or three friends of simple tastes could sit about as they pleased and eat and
smoke and talk in comfort and contentment. The ruddy brick floor smiled up at
the smoky ceiling; the oaken settles, shiny with long wear, exchanged cheerful
glances with each other; plates on the dresser grinned at pots on the shelf, and
the merry firelight flickered and played over everything without distinction.

The kindly Badger thrust them down on a settle to toast themselves at the
fire, and bade them remove their wet coats and boots. Then he fetched them
dressing-gowns and slippers, and himself bathed the Mole's shin with warm
water and mended the cut with sticking-plaster till the whole thing was just as
good as new, if not better. In the embracing light and warmth, warm and
dry at last, with weary legs propped up in front of them, and a suggestive clink
of plates being arranged on the table behind, it seemed to the storm-driven

animals, now in safe anchorage, that the cold and trackless Wild Wood just left outside was miles and miles away, and all that they had suffered in it a half-forgotten dream.

When at last they were thoroughly toasted, the Badger summoned them to the table, where he had been busy laying a repast. They had felt pretty hungry before, but when they actually saw at last the supper that was spread for them, really it seemed only a question of what they should attack first where all was so attractive, and whether the other things would obligingly wait for them till they had time to give them attention. Conversation was impossible for a long time; and when it was slowly resumed, it was that regrettable sort of conversation that results from talking with your mouth full. The Badger did not mind that sort of thing at all, nor did he take any notice of elbows on the table, or everybody speaking at once. As he did not go into Society himself, he had got an idea that these things belonged to the things that didn't really matter. (We know of course that he was wrong, and took too narrow a view; because they do matter very much, though it would take too long to explain why.) He sat in his arm-chair at the head of the table, and nodded gravely at intervals as the animals told their story; and he did not seem surprised or shocked at anything, and he never said, "I told you so," or, "Just what I always said," or remarked that they ought to have done so-and-so, or ought not to have done something else. The Mole began to feel very friendly towards him.

When supper was really finished at last, and each animal felt that his skin was now tight as was decently safe, and that by this time he didn't care a hang for anybody or anything, they gathered round the glowing embers of the great wood fire, and thought how jolly it was to be sitting up *so* late, and *so* independent, and *so* full; and after they had chatted for a time about things in general, the Badger said heartily, "Now then! tell us the news from your part of the world. How's old Toad going on?"

"O, from bad to worse," said the Rat gravely, while the Mole, cocked up on a settle and basking in the firelight, his heels higher than his head, tried to look properly mournful. "Another smash-up only last week, and a bad one. You see, he will insist on driving himself, and he's hopelessly incapable. If he'd only employ a decent, steady, well-trained animal, pay him good wages, and leave everything to him, he'd get on all right. But no; he's convinced he's a heaven-born driver, and nobody can teach him anything; and all the rest follows."

"How many has he had?" inquired the Badger gloomily.

"Smashes, or machines?" asked the Rat. "O, well, after all, it's the same thing – with Toad. This is the seventh. As for the others – you know that coach-house of his? Well, it's piled up – literally piled up to the roof – with fragments of motor-cars, none of them bigger than your hat! That accounts for the other six – so far as they can be accounted for."

"He's been in hospital three times," put in the Mole; "and as for the fines he's had to pay, it's simply awful to think of."

"Yes, and that's part of the trouble," continued the Rat. "Toad's rich, we all know; but he's not a millionaire. And he's a hopelessly bad driver, and quite regardless of law and order. Killed or ruined – it's got to be one of the two things, sooner or later. Badger! we're his friends – oughtn't we to do something?"

The Badger went through a bit of hard thinking. "Now look here!" he said at last, rather severely; "of course you know I can't do anything *now?*"

His two friends assented, quite understanding his point. No animal, according to the rules of animal-etiquette, is ever expected to do anything strenuous, or heroic, or even moderately active during the off-season of winter. All are sleepy – some actually asleep. All are weather-bound, more or less; and all are resting from arduous days and nights, during which every muscle in them has been severely tested, and every energy kept at full stretch.

"Very well then!" continued the Badger. "*But,* when once the year has really turned, and the nights are shorter, and half-way through them one rouses and feels fidgety and wanting to be up and doing by sunrise, if not before – *you* know! –"

Both animals nodded gravely. *They* knew!

"Well, *then,*" went on the Badger, "we – that is, you and me and our friend the Mole here – we'll take Toad seriously in hand. We'll stand no nonsense whatever. We'll bring him back to reason, by force if need be. We'll *make* him be a sensible Toad. We'll – you're asleep, Rat!"

"Not me!" said the Rat, waking up with a jerk.

"He's been asleep two or three times since supper," said the Mole, laughing. He himself was feeling quite wakeful and even lively, though he didn't know why. The reason was, of course, that he being naturally an underground animal by birth and breeding, the situation of Badger's house exactly suited him and made him feel at home; while the Rat, who slept every night in a bedroom the windows of which opened on a breezy river, naturally felt the atmosphere still and oppressive.

"Well, it's time we were all in bed," said the Badger, getting up and fetching flat candlesticks. "Come along, you two, and I'll show you your quarters. And take your time to-morrow morning – breakfast at any hour you please!"

He conducted the two animals to a long room that seemed half bedchamber and half loft. The Badger's winter stores, which indeed were visible everywhere, took up half the room – piles of apples, turnips, and potatoes, baskets full of nuts, and jars of honey; but the two little white beds on the remainder of the floor looked soft and inviting, and the linen on them, though coarse, was clean and smelt beautifully of lavender; and the Mole and the Water Rat, shaking off their garments in some thirty seconds, tumbled in between the sheets in great joy and contentment.

In accordance with the kindly Badger's injunctions, the two tired animals came down to breakfast very late next morning, and found a bright fire burning in the kitchen, and two young hedgehogs sitting on a bench at the table, eating oatmeal porridge out of wooden bowls. The hedgehogs dropped their spoons, rose to their feet, and ducked their heads respectfully as the two entered.

"There, sit down, sit down," said the Rat pleasantly, "and go on with your porridge. Where have you youngsters come from? Lost your way in the snow, I suppose?"

"Yes, please, sir," said the elder of the two hedgehogs respectfully. "Me and little Billy here, we was trying to find our way to school – mother *would* have us go, was the weather ever so – and of course we lost ourselves, sir, and Billy he got frightened and took and cried, being young and faint-hearted. And at last we happened up against Mr Badger's back door, and made so bold as to knock, sir, for Mr Badger he's a kind-hearted gentleman, as everyone knows –"

"I understand," said the Rat, cutting himself some rashers from a side of bacon, while the Mole dropped some eggs into a saucepan. "And what's the weather like outside? You needn't 'sir' me quite so much," he added.

"O, terrible bad, sir, terrible deep the snow is," said the hedgehog. "No getting out for the likes of you gentlemen to-day."

"Where's Mr Badger?" inquired the Mole, as he warmed the coffee-pot before the fire.

"The master's gone into his study, sir," replied the hedgehog, "and he said as how he was going to be particular busy this morning, and on no account was he to be disturbed."

This explanation, of course, was thoroughly understood by everyone present. The fact is, as already set forth, when you live a life of intense activity for six months in the year, and of comparative or actual somnolence for the other six, during the latter period you cannot be continually pleading sleepiness when there are people about or things to be done. The excuse gets monotonous. The animals well knew that Badger, having eaten a hearty breakfast, had retired to his study and settled in an arm-chair with his legs up on another and a red cotton handkerchief over his face, and was being "busy" in the usual way at this time of the year.

The front-door bell clanged loudly, and the Rat, who was very greasy with buttered toast, sent Billy, the smaller hedgehog, to see who it might be. There was a sound of much stamping in the hall, and presently Billy returned in front of the Otter, who threw himself on the Rat with an embrace and a shout of affectionate greeting.

"Get off!" spluttered the Rat, with his mouth full.

"Thought I should find you here all right," said the Otter cheerfully. "They were all in a great state of alarm along River Bank when I arrived this morning. Rat never been home all night – nor Mole either – something dreadful must have happened, they said; and the snow had covered up all your tracks, of course. But I knew that when people were in any fix they mostly went to Badger, or else Badger got to know of it somehow, so I came straight off here, through the Wild Wood and the snow! My! it was fine, coming through the snow as the red sun was rising and showing against the black tree-trunks! As you went along in the stillness, every now and then masses of snow slid off the branches suddenly with a flop! making you jump and run for cover. Snow-castles and snow-caverns had sprung up out of nowhere in the night – and snow bridges, terraces, ramparts – I could have stayed and played with them for hours. Here and there great branches had been torn away by the sheer weight of the snow, and robins perched and hopped on them in their perky conceited way just as if they had done it themselves. A ragged string of wild geese passed overhead, high on the grey sky, and a few rooks whirled over the trees, inspected, and flapped off homewards with a disgusted expression; but I met no sensible being to ask the news of. About half-way across I came on a rabbit sitting on a stump, cleaning his silly face with his paws. He was a pretty scared animal when I crept up behind him and placed a heavy fore-paw on his shoulder. I had to cuff his head once or twice to get any sense out of it at all. At last I managed to extract from him that Mole had been seen in the Wild Wood last night by one of them. It was the talk of the burrows, he said, how Mole, Mr Rat's particular friend, was in a bad fix; how he had lost his way, and 'They' were up and out hunting, and were chivvying him round and round. 'Then why didn't any of you *do* something?' I asked. 'You mayn't be blest with brains, but there are hundreds and hundreds of you, big stout fellows, as fat as butter, and your burrows running in all directions, and you could have taken him in and made him safe and comfortable, or tried to, at all events.' 'What, *us?*' he merely said: '*do* something? us rabbits?' So I cuffed him again and left him. There was nothing else to be done. At any rate, I had learnt something; and if I had had the luck to meet any of 'Them' I'd have learnt something more – or *they* would."

"Weren't you at all – er – nervous?" asked the Mole, some of yesterday's terror coming back to him at the mention of the Wild Wood.

"Nervous?" The Otter showed a gleaming set of strong white teeth as he laughed. "I'd give 'em nerves if any of them tried anything on with me. Here, Mole, fry me some slices of ham, like the good little chap you are. I'm frightfully hungry, and I've got any amount to say to Ratty here. Haven't seen him for an age."

So the good-natured Mole, having cut some slices of ham, set the hedgehogs to fry it, and returned to his own breakfast, while the Otter and the Rat, their heads together, eagerly talked river-shop, which is long shop and talk that is endless, running on like the babbling river itself.

A plate of fried ham had just been cleared and sent back for more, when the Badger entered, yawning and rubbing his eyes, and greeted them all in his quiet, simple way, with kind inquiries for everyone. "It must be getting on for luncheon time," he remarked to the Otter. "Better stop and have it with us. You must be hungry, this cold morning."

"Rather!" replied the Otter, winking at the Mole. "The sight of these greedy young hedgehogs stuffing themselves with fried ham makes me feel positively famished."

The hedgehogs, who were just beginning to feel hungry again after their porridge, and after working so hard at their frying, looked timidly up at Mr Badger, but were too shy to say anything.

"Here, you two youngsters, be off home to your mother," said the Badger kindly. "I'll send someone with you to show you the way. You won't want any dinner to-day, I'll be bound."

He gave them sixpence apiece and a pat on the head, and they went off with much respectful swinging of caps and touching of forelocks.

Presently they all sat down to luncheon together. The Mole found himself placed next to Mr Badger, and, as the other two were still deep in river-gossip from which nothing could divert them, he took the opportunity to tell Badger how comfortable and home-like it all felt to him. "Once well underground," he said, "you know exactly where you are. Nothing can happen to you, and nothing can get at you. You're entirely your own master, and you don't have to consult anybody or mind what they say. Things go on all the same overhead, and you let 'em, and don't bother about 'em. When you want to, up you go, and there the things are, waiting for you."

The Badger simply beamed on him. "That's exactly what I say," he replied. "There's no security, or peace and tranquillity, except underground. And then, if your ideas get larger and you want to expand – why, a dig and a scrape and there you are! If you feel your house is a bit too big, you stop up a hole or two, and there you are again! No builders, no tradesmen, no remarks passed on you by fellows looking over your wall, and, above all, no *weather*. Look at Rat, now. A couple of feet of flood-water, and he's got to move into hired lodgings; uncomfortable, inconveniently situated, and horribly expensive. Take Toad. I say nothing against Toad Hall; quite the best house in these parts, *as* a house. But supposing a fire breaks out – where's Toad? Supposing tiles are blown off, or walls sink or crack, or windows get broken – where's Toad? Supposing the rooms are draughty – I *hate* a draught myself – where's Toad? No, up and out of doors is good enough to roam about and get one's living in; but underground to come back to at last – that's my idea of *home*!"

The Mole assented heartily; and the Badger in consequence got very friendly with him. "When lunch is over," he said, "I'll take you all round this little place of mine. I can see you'll appreciate it. You understand what domestic architecture ought to be, you do."

After luncheon, accordingly, when the other two had settled themselves into the chimney-corner and had started a heated argument on the subject of *eels*, the Badger lighted a lantern and bade the Mole follow him. Crossing the hall, they passed down one of the principal tunnels, and the wavering light of the lantern gave glimpses on either side of rooms both large and small, some mere cupboards, others nearly as broad and imposing as Toad's dining-hall. A narrow passage at right angles led them into another corridor, and here the same thing was repeated. The Mole was staggered at the size, the extent, the ramifications of it all; at the length of the dim passages, the solid vaultings of the crammed store-chambers, the masonry everywhere, the pillars, the arches, the pavements. "How on earth, Badger," he said at last, "did you ever find time and strength to do all this? It's astonishing!"

"It *would* be astonishing indeed," said the Badger simply, "if I *had* done it.

But as a matter of fact I did none of it – only cleaned out the passages and chambers, as far as I had need of them. There's lots more of it, all round about. I see you don't understand, and I must explain it to you. Well, very long ago, on the spot where the Wild Wood waves now, before ever it had planted itself and grown up to what it now is, there was a city – a city of people, you know. Here, where we are standing, they lived, and walked, and talked, and slept, and carried on their business. Here they stabled their horses and feasted, from here they rode out to fight or drove out to trade. They were a powerful people, and rich, and great builders. They built to last, for they thought their city would last for ever."

"But what has become of them all?" asked the Mole.

"Who can tell?" said the Badger. "People come – they stay for a while, they flourish, they build – and they go. It is their way. But we remain. There were badgers here, I've been told, long before that same city ever came to be. And now there are badgers here again. We are an enduring lot, and we may move out for a time, but we wait, and are patient, and back we come. And so it will ever be."

"Well, and when they went at last, those people?" said the Mole.

"When they went," continued the Badger, "the strong winds and persistent rains took the matter in hand, patiently, ceaselessly, year after year. Perhaps we badgers too, in our small way, helped a little – who knows? It was all down, down, down, gradually – ruin and levelling and disappearance. Then it was all up, up, up, gradually, as seeds grew to saplings, and saplings to forest trees, and bramble and fern came creeping in to help. Leaf-mould rose and obliterated, streams in their winter freshets brought sand and soil to clog and to cover, and in course of time our home was ready for us again, and we moved in. Up above us, on the surface, the same thing happened. Animals arrived, liked the look of the place, took up their quarters, settled down, spread, and flourished. They didn't bother themselves about the past – they never do; they're too busy. The place was a bit humpy and hillocky, naturally, and full of holes; but that was rather an advantage. And they don't bother about the future, either – the future when perhaps the people will move in again – for a time – as may very well be. The Wild Wood is pretty well populated by now; with all the usual lot, good, bad, and indifferent – I name no names. It takes all sorts to make a world. But I fancy you know something about them yourself by this time."

"I do indeed," said the Mole, with a slight shiver.

"Well, well," said the Badger, patting him on the shoulder, "it was your first experience of them, you see. They're not so bad really; and we must all live and let live. But I'll pass the word round to-morrow, and I think you'll have no further trouble. Any friend of *mine* walks where he likes in this country, or I'll know the reason why!"

When they got back to the kitchen again, they found the Rat walking up and down, very restless. The underground atmosphere was oppressing him and getting on his nerves, and he seemed really to be afraid that the river would run away if he wasn't there to look after it. So he had his overcoat on, and his pistols thrust into his belt again. "Come along, Mole," he said anxiously, as soon as he caught sight of them. "We must get off while it's daylight. Don't want to spend another night in the Wild Wood again."

"It'll be all right, my fine fellow," said the Otter. "I'm coming along with you, and I know every path blindfold; and if there's a head that needs to be punched, you can confidently rely upon me to punch it."

"You really needn't fret, Ratty," added the Badger placidly. "My passages run further than you think, and I've bolt-holes to the edge of the wood in several directions, though I don't care for everybody to know about them. When you really have to go, you shall leave by one of my short cuts. Meantime, make yourself easy, and sit down again."

The Rat was nevertheless still anxious to be off and attend to his river, so the Badger, taking up his lantern again, led the way along a damp and airless tunnel that wound and dipped, part vaulted, part hewn through solid rock, for a weary distance that seemed to be miles. At last daylight began to show itself confusedly through tangled growth overhanging the mouth of the passage; and the Badger, bidding them a hasty good-bye, pushed them hurriedly through the opening, made everything look as natural as possible again, with creepers, brushwood, and dead leaves, and retreated.

They found themselves standing on the very edge of the Wild Wood.

Rocks and brambles and tree-roots behind them, confusedly heaped and tangled; in front, a great space of quiet fields, hemmed by lines of hedges black on the snow, and, far ahead, a glint of the familiar old river, while the wintry sun hung red and low on the horizon. The Otter, as knowing all the paths, took charge of the party, and they trailed out on a bee-line for a distant stile. Pausing there a moment and looking back, they saw the whole mass of the Wild Wood, dense, menacing, compact, grimly set in vast white surroundings; simultaneously they turned and made swiftly for home, for firelight and the familiar things it played on, for the voice, sounding cheerily outside their window, of the river that they knew and trusted in all its moods, that never made them afraid with any amazement.

As he hurried along, eagerly anticipating the moment when he would be at home again among the things he knew and liked, the Mole saw clearly that he was an animal of tilled field and hedgerow, linked to the ploughed furrow, the frequented pasture, the lane of evening lingerings, the cultivated garden-plot. For others the asperities, the stubborn endurance, or the clash of actual conflict, that went with Nature in the rough; he must be wise, must keep to the pleasant places in which his lines were laid and which held adventure enough, in their way, to last for a lifetime.

Chapter 5

Dulce Domum

The sheep ran huddling together against the hurdles, blowing out thin nostrils and stamping with delicate fore-feet, their heads thrown back and a light steam rising from the crowded sheep-pen into the frosty air, as the two animals hastened by in high spirits, with much chatter and laughter. They were returning across country after a long day's outing with Otter, hunting and exploring on the wide uplands where certain streams tributary to their own river had their first small beginnings; and the shades of the short winter day were closing in on them, and they had still some distance to go. Plodding at random across the plough, they had heard the sheep and had made for them; and now, leading from the sheep-pen, they found a beaten track that made walking a lighter business, and responded, moreover, to that small inquiring something which all animals carry inside them, saying unmistakably, "Yes, quite right; *this* leads home!"

"It looks as if we were coming to a village," said the Mole somewhat dubiously, slackening his pace, as the track, that had in time become a path and then had developed into a lane, now handed them over to the charge of a well-metalled road. The animals did not hold with villages, and their own highways, thickly frequented as they were, took an independent course, regardless of church, post office, or public-house.

"Oh, never mind!" said the Rat. "At this season of the year they're all safe indoors by this time, sitting round the fire; men, women, and children, dogs and cats and all. We shall slip through all right, without any bother or unpleasantness, and we can have a look at them through their windows if you like, and see what they're doing."

The rapid nightfall of mid-December had quite beset the little village as they approached it on soft feet over a first thin fall of powdery snow. Little was visible but squares of a dusky orange-red on either side of the street, where the firelight or lamplight of each cottage overflowed through the casements into the dark world without. Most of the low latticed windows were innocent of blinds, and to the lookers-in from outside, the inmates, gathered round the tea-table, absorbed in handiwork, or talking with laughter and gesture, had each that happy grace which is the last thing the skilled actor shall capture – the natural grace which goes with perfect unconsciousness of observation. Moving at will from one theatre to another, the two spectators, so far from home themselves, had something of wistfulness in their eyes as they watched a cat being stroked, a sleepy child picked up and huddled off to bed, or a tired man stretch and knock out his pipe on the end of a smouldering log.

But it was from one little window, with its blind drawn down, a mere blank transparency on the night, that the sense of home and the little curtained world within walls – the larger stressful world of outside Nature shut out and forgotten – most pulsated. Close against the white blind hung a bird-cage, clearly silhouetted, every wire, perch, and appurtenance distinct and recognizable, even to yesterday's dull-edged lump of sugar. On the middle perch the fluffy occupant, head tucked well into feathers, seemed so near to them as to be easily stroked, had they tried; even the delicate tips of his plumped-out plumage pencilled plainly on the illuminated screen. As they looked, the sleepy little fellow stirred uneasily, woke, shook himself, and raised his head. They could see the gape of his tiny beak as he yawned in a bored sort of way, looked round, and then settled his head into his back again, while the ruffled feathers gradually subsided into perfect stillness. Then a gust of bitter wind took them in the back of the neck, a small sting of frozen sleet on the skin woke them as from a dream, and they knew their toes to be cold and their legs tired, and their own home distant a weary way.

Once beyond the village, where the cottages ceased abruptly, on either side of the road they could smell through the darkness the friendly fields again; and they braced themselves for the last long stretch, the home stretch, the stretch that we know is bound to end, some time, in the rattle of the door-latch, the sudden firelight, and the sight of familiar things greeting us as long-absent travellers from far oversea. They plodded along steadily and silently, each of them thinking his own thoughts. The Mole's ran a good deal on supper, as it was pitch-dark, and it was all a strange country to him as far as he knew, and he was following obediently in the wake of the Rat, leaving the guidance entirely to him. As for the Rat, he was walking a little way ahead, as his habit was, his shoulders humped, his eyes fixed on the straight grey road in front of him; so he did not notice poor Mole when suddenly the summons reached him, and took him like an electric shock.

We others, who have long lost the more subtle of the physical senses, have not even proper terms to express an animal's intercommunications with his surroundings, living or otherwise, and have only the word "smell," for instance, to include the whole range of delicate thrills which murmur in the nose of the animal night and day, summoning, warning, inciting, repelling. It was one of these mysterious fairy calls from out the void that suddenly reached Mole in the darkness, making him tingle through and through with its very familiar appeal, even while as yet he could not clearly remember what it was. He stopped dead in his tracks, his nose searching hither and thither in its efforts to recapture the fine filament, the telegraphic current, that had so strongly moved him. A moment, and he had caught it again; and with it this time came recollection in fullest flood.

Home! That was what they meant, those caressing appeals, those soft touches wafted through the air, those invisible little hands pulling and tugging, all one way! Why, it must be quite close by him at that moment, his old home that he had hurriedly forsaken and never sought again, that day when he first found the river! And now it was sending out its scouts and its messengers to capture him and bring him in. Since his escape on that bright morning he had hardly given it a thought, so absorbed had he been in his new life, in all its pleasures, its surprises, its fresh and captivating experiences. Now, with a rush of old memories, how clearly it stood up before him, in the darkness! Shabby indeed, and small and poorly furnished, and yet his, the home he had made for himself, the home he had been so happy to get back to after his day's work. And the home had been happy with him, too, evidently, and was missing him, and wanted him back, and was telling him so, through his nose, sorrowfully, reproachfully, but with no bitterness or anger; only with plaintive reminder that it was there, and wanted him.

The call was clear, the summons was plain. He must obey it instantly, and go. "Ratty!" he called, full of joyful excitement, "hold on! Come back! I want you, quick!"

"O, *come* along, Mole, do!" replied the Rat cheerfully, still plodding **along**.

"*Please* stop, Ratty!" pleaded the poor Mole, in anguish of heart. "You don't understand! It's my home, my old home! I've just come across the smell of it, and it's close by here, really quite close. And I *must* go to it, I must, I must! O, come back, Ratty! Please, please come back!"

The Rat was by this time very far ahead, too far to hear clearly what the Mole was calling, too far to catch the sharp note of painful appeal in his voice. And he was much taken up with the weather, for he too could smell something – something suspiciously like approaching snow.

"Mole, we mustn't stop now, really!" he called back. "We'll come for it to-morrow, whatever it is you've found. But I daren't stop now – it's late, and the snow's coming on again, and I'm not sure of the way! And I want your nose, Mole, so come on quick, there's a good fellow!" And the Rat pressed forward on his way without waiting for an answer.

Poor Mole stood alone in the road, his heart torn asunder and a big sob gathering, gathering, somewhere low down inside him, to leap up to the surface presently, he knew, in passionate escape. But even under such a test as this his loyalty to his friend stood firm. Never for a moment did he dream of abandoning him. Meanwhile, the wafts from his old home pleaded, whispered, conjured, and finally claimed him imperiously. He dared not tarry longer within their magic circle. With a wrench that tore his very heartstrings he set his face down the road and followed submissively in the track of the Rat, while faint, thin little smells, still dogging his retreating nose, reproached him for his new friendship and his callous forgetfulness.

With an effort he caught up the unsuspecting Rat, who began chattering cheerfully about what they would do when they got back, and how jolly a fire of logs in the parlour would be, and what a supper he meant to eat; never noticing his companion's silence and distressful state of mind. At last, however, when they had gone some considerable way further, and were passing some tree-stumps at the edge of a copse that bordered the road, he stopped and said kindly, "Look here, Mole, old chap, you seem dead tired. No talk left in you, and your feet dragging like lead. We'll sit down here for a minute and rest. The snow has held off so far, and the best part of our journey is over."

The Mole subsided forlornly on a tree-stump and tried to control himself, for he felt it surely coming. The sob he had fought with so long refused to be beaten. Up and up, it forced its way to the air, and then another, and another, and others thick and fast; till poor Mole at last gave up the struggle, and cried freely and helplessly and openly, now that he knew it was all over and he had lost what he could hardly be said to have found.

The Rat, astonished and dismayed at the violence of Mole's paroxysm of grief, did not dare to speak for a while. At last he said, very quietly and sympathetically, "What is it, old fellow? Whatever can be the matter? Tell us your trouble, and let me see what I can do."

Poor Mole found it difficult to get any words out between the upheavals of his chest that followed one upon another so quickly and held back speech and choked it as it came. "I know it's a – shabby, dingy little place," he sobbed forth at last, brokenly: "not like – your cosy quarters – or Toad's beautiful hall – or

Badger's great house – but it was my own little home – and I was fond of it – and I went away and forgot all about it – and then I smelt it suddenly – on the road, when I called and you wouldn't listen, Rat – and everything came back to me with a rush – and I *wanted* it! – O dear, O dear! – and when you *wouldn't* turn back, Ratty – and I had to leave it, though I was smelling it all the time – I thought my heart would break. – We might have just gone and had one look at it, Ratty – only one look – it was close by – but you wouldn't turn back, Ratty, you wouldn't turn back! O dear, O dear!"

Recollection brought fresh waves of sorrow, and sobs again took full charge of him, preventing further speech.

The Rat stared straight in front of him, saying nothing, only patting Mole gently on the shoulder. After a time he muttered gloomily, "I see it all now! What a *pig* I have been! A pig – that's me! Just a pig – a plain pig!"

He waited till Mole's sobs became gradually less stormy and more rhythmical; he waited till at last sniffs were frequent and sobs only intermittent. Then he rose from his seat, and, remarking carelessly, "Well, now we'd really better be getting on, old chap!" set off up the road again, over the toilsome way they had come.

"Wherever are you (hic) going to (hic), Ratty?" cried the tearful Mole, looking up in alarm.

"We're going to find that home of yours, old fellow," replied the Rat pleasantly; "so you had better come along, for it will take some finding, and we shall want your nose."

"O, come back, Ratty, do!" cried the Mole, getting up and hurrying after him. "It's no good, I tell you! It's too late, and too dark, and the place is too far off, and the snow's coming! And – and I never meant to let you know I was feeling that way about it – it was all an accident and a mistake! And think of River Bank, and your supper!"

"Hang River Bank, and supper too!" said the Rat heartily. "I tell you, I'm going to find this place now, if I stay out all night. So cheer up, old chap, and take my arm, and we'll very soon be back there again."

Still snuffling, pleading, and reluctant, Mole suffered himself to be dragged back along the road by his imperious companion, who by a flow of cheerful talk and anecdote endeavoured to beguile his spirits back and make the weary way seem shorter. When at last it seemed to the Rat that they must be nearing that part of the road where the Mole had been "held up", he said, "Now, no more talking. Business! Use your nose, and give your mind to it."

They moved on in silence for some little way, when suddenly the Rat was conscious, through his arm that was linked in Mole's, of a faint sort of electric thrill that was passing down that animal's body. Instantly he disengaged himself, fell back a pace, and waited, all attention.

The signals were coming through!

Mole stood a moment rigid, while his uplifted nose, quivering slightly, felt the air.

Then a short, quick run forward – a fault – a check – a try back; and then a slow, steady, confident advance.

The Rat, much excited, kept close to his heels as the Mole, with something of the air of a sleep-walker, crossed a dry ditch, scrambled through a hedge, and nosed his way over a field open and trackless and bare in the faint starlight.

Suddenly, without giving warning, he dived; but the Rat was on the alert, and promptly followed him down the tunnel to which his unerring nose had faithfully led him.

It was close and airless, and the earthy smell was strong, and it seemed a long time to Rat ere the passage ended and he could stand erect and stretch and shake himself. The Mole struck a match, and by its light the Rat saw that they were standing in an open space, neatly swept and sanded underfoot, and directly facing them was Mole's little front door, with "Mole End" painted, in Gothic lettering, over the bell-pull at the side.

Mole reached down a lantern from a nail on the wall and lit it, and the Rat, looking round him, saw that they were in a sort of fore-court. A garden-seat stood on one side of the door, and on the other, a roller; for the Mole, who was a tidy animal when at home, could not stand having his ground kicked up by other animals into little runs that ended in earth-heaps. On the walls hung wire baskets with ferns in them, alternating with brackets carrying plaster statuary – Garibaldi, and the infant Samuel, and Queen Victoria, and other heroes of modern Italy. Down one side of the fore-court ran a skittle-alley, with benches along it and little wooden tables marked with rings that hinted at beer-mugs. In the middle was a small round pond containing goldfish and surrounded by a cockle-shell border. Out of the centre of the pond rose a fanciful erection clothed in more cockle-shells and topped by a large silvered glass ball that reflected everything all wrong and had a very pleasing effect.

Mole's face beamed at the sight of all these objects so dear to him, and he hurried Rat through the door, lit a lamp in the hall, and took one glance round his old home. He saw the dust lying thick on everything, saw the cheerless, deserted look of the long-neglected house, and its narrow, meagre dimensions, its worn and shabby contents – and collapsed again on a hall-chair, his nose in his paws. "O, Ratty!" he cried dismally, "why ever did I do it? Why did I bring you to this poor, cold little place, on a night like this, when you might have been at River Bank by this time, toasting your toes before a blazing fire, with all your own nice things about you!"

The Rat paid no heed to his doleful self-reproaches. He was running here and there, opening doors, inspecting rooms and cupboards, and lighting lamps and candles and sticking them up everywhere. "What a capital little house this is!" he called out cheerily. "So compact! So well planned! Everything here and everything in its place! We'll make a jolly night of it. The first thing we want is a good fire; I'll see to that – I always know where to find things. So this is the parlour? Splendid! Your own idea, those little sleeping-bunks in the wall? Capital! Now, I'll fetch the wood and the coals, and you get a duster, Mole – you'll find one in the drawer of the kitchen table – and try and smarten things up a bit. Bustle about, old chap!"

Encouraged by his inspiriting companion, the Mole roused himself and dusted and polished with energy and heartiness, while the Rat, running to and fro with armfuls of fuel, soon had a cheerful blaze roaring up the chimney. He hailed the Mole to come and warm himself; but Mole promptly had another fit of the blues, dropping down on a couch in dark despair and burying his face in his duster. "Rat," he moaned, "how about your supper, you poor, cold, hungry, weary animal? I've nothing to give you – nothing – not a crumb!"

"What a fellow you are for giving in!" said the Rat reproachfully. "Why, only just now I saw a sardine-opener on the kitchen dresser, quite distinctly; and everybody knows that means there are sardines about somewhere in the neighbourhood. Rouse yourself! pull yourself together, and come with me and forage."

They went and foraged accordingly, hunting through every cupboard and turning out every drawer. The result was not so very depressing after all, though of course it might have been better; a tin of sardines – a box of captain's biscuits, nearly full – and a German sausage encased in silver paper.

"There's a banquet for you!" observed the Rat, as he arranged the table. "I know some animals who would give their ears to be sitting down to supper with us to-night!"

"No bread!" groaned the Mole dolorously; "no butter, no –"

"No *pâté de foie gras*, no champagne!" continued the Rat, grinning. "And that reminds me – what's that little door at the end of the passage? Your cellar, of course! Every luxury in this house! Just you wait a minute."

He made for the cellar door, and presently reappeared, somewhat dusty, with a bottle of beer in each paw and another under each arm. "Self-indulgent beggar you seem to be, Mole," he observed. "Deny yourself nothing. This is really the jolliest little place I ever was in. Now, wherever did you pick up those prints? Make the place look so home-like, they do. No wonder you're so fond of it, Mole. Tell us all about it, and how you came to make it what it is."

Then, while the Rat busied himself fetching plates, and knives and forks, and mustard which he mixed in an egg-cup, the Mole, his bosom still heaving with the stress of his recent emotion, related – somewhat shyly at first, but with more freedom as he warmed to his subject – how this was planned, and how that was thought out, and how this was got through a windfall from an aunt, and that was a wonderful find and a bargain, and this other thing was bought out of laborious savings and a certain amount of "going without". His spirits finally quite restored, he must needs go and caress his possessions, and take a lamp and show off their points to his visitor and expatiate on them, quite forgetful of the supper they both so much needed; Rat, who was desperately hungry but strove to conceal it, nodding seriously, examining with a puckered brow, and saying, "Wonderful," and "Most remarkable," at intervals, when the chance for an observation was given him.

At last the Rat succeeded in decoying him to the table, and had just got seriously to work with the sardine-opener when sounds were heard from the fore-court without – sounds like the scuffling of small feet in the gravel and a confused murmur of tiny voices, while broken sentences reached them – "Now, all in a line – hold the lantern up a bit, Tommy – clear your throats first – no coughing after I say one, two, three. – Where's young Bill? – Here, come on, do, we're all a-waiting –"

"What's up?" inquired the Rat, pausing in his labours.

"I think it must be the field-mice," replied the Mole, with a touch of pride in his manner. "They go round carol-singing regularly at this time of the year. They're quite an institution in these parts. And they never pass me over – they come to Mole End last of all; and I used to give them hot drinks, and supper too sometimes, when I could afford it. It will be like old times to hear them again."

"Let's have a look at them!" cried the Rat, jumping up and running to the door.

It was a pretty sight, and a seasonable one, that met their eyes when they flung the door open. In the fore-court, lit by the dim rays of a horn lantern, some eight or ten little field-mice stood in a semi-circle, red worsted comforters round their throats, their fore-paws thrust deep into their pockets, their feet jigging for warmth. With bright beady eyes they glanced shyly at each other, sniggering a little, sniffing and applying coat-sleeves a good deal. As the door opened, one of the elder ones that carried the lantern was just saying, "Now then, one, two, three!" and forthwith their shrill little voices uprose on the air, singing one of the old-time carols that their forefathers composed in fields that were fallow and held by frost, or when snow-bound in chimney corners, and handed down to be sung in the miry street to lamp-lit windows at Yule-time.

CAROL

Villagers all, this frosty tide,
Let your doors swing open wide,
Though wind may follow, and snow beside,
Yet draw us in by your fire to bide;
    Joy shall be yours in the morning!

Here we stand in the cold and the sleet,
Blowing fingers and stamping feet,
Come from far away you to greet –
You by the fire and we in the street –
    Bidding you joy in the morning!

For ere one half of the night was gone,
Sudden a star has led us on,
Raining bliss and benison –
Bliss to-morrow and more anon,
    Joy for every morning!

Goodman Joseph toiled through the snow –
Saw the star o'er a stable low;
Mary she might not further go –
Welcome thatch, and litter below!
    Joy was hers in the morning!

And then they heard the angels tell
'Who were the first to cry Nowell?
Animals all, as it befell,
In the stable where they did dwell!
Joy shall be theirs in the morning!'

The voices ceased, the singers, bashful but smiling, exchanged sidelong glances, and silence succeeded – but for a moment only. Then, from up above and far away, down the tunnel they had so lately travelled was borne to their ears in a faint musical hum the sound of distant bells ringing a joyful and clangorous peal.

"Very well sung, boys!" cried the Rat heartily. "And now come along in, all of you, and warm yourselves by the fire, and have something hot!"

"Yes, come along, field-mice," cried the Mole eagerly. "This is quite like old times! Shut the door after you. Pull up that settle to the fire. Now, you just wait a minute, while we – O, Ratty!" he cried in despair, plumping down on a seat, with tears impending. "Whatever are we doing? We've nothing to give them!"

"You leave all that to me," said the masterful Rat. "Here, you with the lantern! Come over this way. I want to talk to you. Now, tell me, are there any shops open at this hour of the night?"

"Why, certainly, sir," replied the field-mouse respectfully. "At this time of the year our shops keep open to all sorts of hours."

"Then look here!" said the Rat. "You go off at once, you and your lantern, and you get me –"

Here much muttered conversation ensued, and the Mole only heard bits of it, such as – "Fresh, mind! – no, a pound of that will do – see you get Buggins's, for I won't have any other – no, only the best – if you can't get it there, try somewhere else – yes, of course, home-made, no tinned stuff – well then, do the best you can!" Finally, there was a chink of coins passing from paw to paw, the field-mouse was provided with an ample basket for his purchases, and off he hurried, he and his lantern.

The rest of the field-mice, perched in a row on the settle, their small legs swinging, gave themselves up to enjoyment of the fire, and toasted their chilblains till they tingled; while the Mole, failing to draw them into easy conversation, plunged into family history and made each of them recite the names of his numerous brothers who were too young, it appeared, to be allowed to go out a-carolling this year, but looked forward very shortly to winning the parental consent.

The Rat, meanwhile, was busy examining the label on one of the beer-bottles. "I perceive this to be Old Burton," he remarked approvingly. "*Sensible* Mole! The very thing! Now we shall be able to mull some ale! Get the things ready, Mole, while I draw the corks."

It did not take long to prepare the brew and thrust the tin heater well into the red heart of the fire; and soon every field-mouse was sipping and coughing and choking (for a little mulled ale goes a long way) and wiping his eyes and laughing and forgetting he had ever been cold in all his life.

"They act plays too, these fellows," the Mole explained to the Rat. "Make them up all by themselves, and act them afterwards. And very well they do it, too! They gave us a capital one last year, about a field-mouse who was captured at sea by a Barbary corsair, and made to row in a galley; and when he escaped and got home again, his lady-love had gone into a convent. Here, *you*! You were in it, I remember. Get up and recite a bit."

The field-mouse addressed got up on his legs, giggled shyly, looked round the room, and remained absolutely tongue-tied. His comrades cheered him on, Mole coaxed and encouraged him, and the Rat went so far as

to take him by the shoulders
and shake him; but nothing
could overcome his stage-
fright. They were all
busily engaged on him
like water men applying
the Royal Humane
Society's regulation to a
case of long submersion,
when the latch clicked, the
door opened, and the field-
mouse with the lantern
reappeared, staggering under the
weight of his basket.

There was no more talk of play-acting once the very real and solid contents
of the basket had been tumbled out on the table. Under the generalship of Rat,
everybody was set to do something or to fetch something. In a very few minutes
supper was ready, and Mole, as he took the head of the table in a sort of a dream,
saw a lately barren board set thick with savoury comforts; saw his little friends'
faces brighten and beam as they fell to without delay; and then let himself loose
– for he was famished indeed – on the provender so magically provided, thinking
what a happy home-coming this had turned out, after all. As they ate, they
talked of old times, and the field-mice gave him the local gossip up to date, and
answered as well as they could the hundred questions he had to ask them. The
Rat said little or nothing, only taking care that each guest had what he wanted,
and plenty of it, and that Mole had no trouble or anxiety about anything.

They clattered off at last, very grateful and showering wishes of the season,
with their jacket pockets stuffed with remembrances for the small brothers and

sisters at home. When the door had closed on the last of them and the chink of the lanterns had died away, Mole and Rat kicked the fire up, drew their chairs in, brewed themselves a last nightcap of mulled ale, and discussed the events of the long day. At last the Rat, with a tremendous yawn, said, "Mole, old chap, I'm ready to drop. Sleepy is simply not the word. That your own bunk over on that side? Very well, then, I'll take this. What a ripping little house this is! Everything so handy!"

He clambered into his bunk and rolled himself well up in the blankets, and slumber gathered him forthwith, as a swath of barley is folded into the arms of the reaping-machine.

The weary Mole also was glad to turn in without delay, and soon had his head on his pillow, in great joy and contentment. But ere he closed his eyes he let them wander round his old room, mellow in the glow of the firelight that played or rested on familiar and friendly things which had long been unconsciously a part of him, and now smilingly received him back, without rancour. He was now in just the frame of mind that the tactful Rat had quietly worked to bring about in him. He saw clearly how plain and simple – how narrow, even – it all was; but clearly, too, how much it all meant to him, and the special value of some such anchorage in one's existence. He did not at all want to abandon the new life and its splendid spaces, to turn his back on sun and air and all they offered him and creep home and stay there; the upper world was all too strong, it called to him still, even down there, and he knew he must return to the larger stage. But it was good to think he had this to come back to, this place which was all his own, these things which were so glad to see him again and could always be counted upon for the same simple welcome.

Chapter 6

Mr Toad

It was a bright morning in the early part of summer; the river had resumed its wonted banks and its accustomed pace, and a hot sun seemed to be pulling everything green and bushy and spiky up out of the earth towards him, as if by strings. The Mole and the Water Rat had been up since dawn, very busy on matters connected with boats and the opening of the boating season; painting and varnishing, mending paddles, repairing cushions, hunting for missing boat-hooks, and so on; and were finishing breakfast in their little parlour and eagerly discussing their plans for the day, when a

heavy knock sounded at the door.

"Bother!" said the Rat, all over egg. "See who it is, Mole, like a good chap, since you've finished."

The Mole went to attend the summons, and the Rat heard him utter a cry of surprise. Then he flung the parlour door open, and announced with much importance, "Mr Badger!"

This was a wonderful thing, indeed, that the Badger should pay a formal call on them, or indeed on anybody. He generally had to be caught, if you wanted him badly, as he slipped quietly along a hedgerow of an early morning or a late evening, or else hunted up in his own house in the middle of the wood, which was a serious undertaking.

The Badger strode heavily into the room, and stood looking at the two animals with an expression full of seriousness. The Rat let his egg-spoon fall on the table-cloth, and sat open-mouthed.

"The hour has come!" said the Badger at last with great solemnity.

"What hour?" asked the Rat uneasily, glancing at the clock on the mantelpiece.

"*Whose* hour, you should rather say," replied the Badger. "Why, Toad's hour! The hour of Toad! I said I would take him in hand as soon as the winter was well over, and I'm going to take him in hand to-day!"

"Toad's hour, of course!" cried the Mole delightedly. "Hooray! I remember now! *We'll* teach him to be a sensible Toad!"

"This very morning," continued the Badger, taking an arm-chair, "as I learnt last night from a trustworthy source, another new and exceptionally powerful motor-car will arrive at Toad Hall on approval or return. At this very moment, perhaps, Toad is busy arraying himself in those singularly hideous habiliments so dear to him, which transform him from a (comparatively) good-looking Toad into an Object which throws any decent-minded animal that comes across it into a violent fit. We must be up and doing, ere it is too late. You two animals will accompany me instantly to Toad Hall, and the work of rescue shall be accomplished."

"Right you are!" cried the Rat, starting up. "We'll rescue the poor unhappy animal! We'll convert him! He'll be the most converted Toad that ever was before we've done with him!"

They set off up the road on their mission of mercy, Badger leading the way. Animals when in company walk in a proper and sensible manner, in single file, instead of sprawling all across the road and being of no use or support to each other in case of sudden trouble or danger.

They reached the carriage-drive of Toad Hall to find, as the Badger had anticipated, a shiny new motor-car, of great size, painted a bright red (Toad's favourite colour), standing in front of the house. As they neared the door it was flung open, and Mr Toad, arrayed in goggles, cap, gaiters, and enormous overcoat, came swaggering down the steps, drawing on his gauntleted gloves.

"Hullo! come on, you fellows!" he cried cheerfully on catching sight of them. "You're just in time to come with me for a jolly – to come for a jolly – for a – er – jolly –"

His hearty accents faltered and fell away as he noticed the stern unbending look on the countenances of his silent friends, and his invitation remained unfinished.

The Badger strode up the steps. "Take him inside," he said sternly to his companions. Then, as Toad was hustled through the door, struggling and protesting, he turned to the chauffeur in charge of the new motor-car.

"I'm afraid you won't be wanted to-day," he said. "Mr Toad has changed his mind. He will not require the car. Please understand that this is final. You needn't wait." Then he followed the others inside and shut the door.

"Now, then!" he said to the Toad, when the four of them stood together in the hall, "first of all, take those ridiculous things off!"

"Shan't!" replied Toad, with great spirit. "What is the meaning of this gross outrage? I demand an instant explanation."

"Take them off him, then, you two," ordered the Badger briefly.

They had to lay Toad out on the floor, kicking and calling all sorts of names, before they could get to work properly. Then the Rat sat on him, and the Mole got his motor-clothes off him bit by bit, and they stood him up on his legs again. A good deal of his blustering spirit seemed to have evaporated with the removal of his fine panoply. Now that he was merely Toad, and no longer the Terror of the Highway, he giggled feebly and looked from one to the other appealingly, seeming quite to understand the situation.

"You knew it must come to this, sooner or later, Toad," the Badger explained severely. "You've disregarded all the warnings we've given you, you've gone on squandering the money your father left you, and you're getting us animals a bad name in the district by your furious driving and your smashes and your rows with the police. Independence is all very well, but we animals never allow our friends to make fools of themselves beyond a certain limit; and that limit you've reached. Now, you're a good fellow in many respects, and I don't want to be too hard on you. I'll make one more effort to bring you to reason. You will come with me into the smoking-room, and there you will hear some facts about yourself; and we'll see whether you come out of that room the same Toad that you went in."

He took Toad firmly by the arm, led him into the smoking-room, and closed the door behind them.

"*That's* no good!" said the Rat contemptuously. "*Talking* to Toad'll never cure him. He'll *say* anything."

They made themselves comfortable in arm-chairs and waited patiently. Through the closed door they could just hear the long continuous drone of the Badger's voice, rising and falling in waves of oratory; and presently they noticed that the sermon began to be punctuated at intervals by long-drawn sobs, evidently proceeding from the bosom of Toad, who was a soft-hearted and affectionate fellow, very easily converted – for the time being – to any point of view.

After some three-quarters of an hour the door opened, and the Badger reappeared, solemnly leading by the paw a very limp and dejected Toad. His skin hung baggily about him, his legs wobbled, and his cheeks were furrowed by the tears so plentifully called forth by the Badger's moving discourse.

"Sit down there, Toad," said the Badger kindly, pointing to a chair. "My friends," he went on, "I am pleased to inform you that Toad has at last seen the error of his ways. He is truly sorry for his misguided conduct in the past, and he has undertaken to give up motor-cars entirely and for ever. I have his solemn promise to that effect."

"That is very good news," said the Mole gravely.

"Very good news indeed," observed the Rat dubiously, "if only – *if* only –"

He was looking very hard at Toad as he said this, and could not help thinking he perceived something vaguely resembling a twinkle in that animal's still sorrowful eye.

"There's only one thing more to be done," continued the gratified Badger. "Toad, I want you solemnly to repeat, before your friends here, what you fully admitted to me in the smoking-room just now. First, you are sorry for what you've done, and you see the folly of it all?"

There was a long, long pause. Toad looked desperately this way and that, while the other animals waited in grave silence. At last he spoke.

"No!" he said a little sullenly, but stoutly; "I'm *not* sorry. And it wasn't folly at all! It was simply glorious!"

"What?" cried the Badger, greatly scandalized. "You backsliding animal, didn't you tell me just now, in there –"

"O, yes, yes, in *there*," said Toad impatiently. "I'd have said anything in *there*. You're so eloquent, dear Badger, and so moving, and so convincing, and put all your points so frightfully well – you can do what you like with me in *there*, and you know it. But I've been searching my mind since, and going over things in it, and I find that I'm not a bit sorry or repentant really, so it's no earthly good saying I am; now, is it?"

"Then you don't promise," said the Badger, "never to touch a motor-car again?"

"Certainly not!" replied Toad emphatically. "On the contrary, I faithfully promise that the very first motor-car I see, poop-poop! off I go in it!"

"Told you so, didn't I?" observed the Rat to the Mole.

"Very well, then," said the Badger firmly, rising to his feet. "Since you won't yield to persuasion, we'll try what force can do. I feared it would come to this all along. You've often asked us three to come and stay with you, Toad, in this handsome house of yours; well, now we're going to. When we've converted you to a proper point of view we may quit, but not before. Take him upstairs, you two, and lock him up in his bedroom, while we arrange matters between ourselves."

"It's for your own good, Toady, you know," said the Rat kindly, as Toad, kicking and struggling, was hauled up the stairs by his two faithful friends. "Think what fun we shall all have together, just as we used to, when you've quite got over this – this painful attack of yours!"

"We'll take great care of everything for you till you're well, Toad," said the

Mole; "and we'll see your money isn't wasted, as it has been."

"No more of those regrettable incidents with the police, Toad," said the Rat, as they thrust him into his bedroom.

"And no more weeks in hospital, being ordered about by female nurses, Toad," added the Mole, turning the key on him.

They descended the stair, Toad shouting abuse at them through the keyhole; and the three friends then met in conference on the situation.

"It's going to be a tedious business," said the Badger, sighing. "I've never seen Toad so determined. However, we will see it out. He must never be left an instant unguarded. We shall have to take it in turns to be with him, till the poison has worked itself out of his system."

They arranged watches accordingly. Each animal took it in turns to sleep in Toad's room at night, and they divided the day up between them. At first Toad was undoubtedly very trying to his careful guardians. When his violent paroxysms possessed him he would arrange bedroom chairs in rude resemblance of a motor-car and would crouch on the foremost of them, bent forward and staring fixedly ahead, making uncouth and ghastly noises, till the climax was reached, when, turning a complete somersault, he would lie prostrate amidst the ruins of the chairs, apparently completely satisfied for the moment. As time passed, however, these painful seizures grew gradually less frequent, and his friends strove to divert his mind into fresh channels. But his interest in other matters did not seem to revive, and he grew apparently languid and depressed.

One fine morning the Rat, whose turn it was to go on duty, went upstairs to relieve Badger, whom he found fidgeting to be off and stretch his legs in a long ramble round his wood and down his earths and burrows. "Toad's still in bed," he told the Rat, outside the door. "Can't get much out of him, except, 'O, leave him alone, he wants nothing, perhaps he'll be better presently, it may pass off in time, don't be unduly anxious,' and so on. Now, you look out, Rat! When Toad's quiet and submissive, and playing at being the hero of a Sunday-school prize, then he's at his artfullest. There's sure to be something up. I know him. Well, now I must be off."

"How are you to-day, old chap?" inquired the Rat cheerfully, as he approached Toad's bedside.

He had to wait some minutes for an answer. At last a feeble voice replied, "Thank you so much, dear Ratty! So good of you to inquire! But first tell me how you are yourself, and the excellent Mole?"

"O, *we're* all right," replied the Rat. "Mole," he added incautiously, "is going out for a run round with Badger. They'll be out till luncheon-time, so you and I will spend a pleasant morning together, and I'll do my best to amuse you. Now jump up, there's a good fellow, and don't lie moping there on a fine morning like this!"

"Dear, kind Rat," murmured Toad, "how little you realize my condition, and how very far I am from 'jumping up' now – if ever! But do not trouble about me. I hate being a burden to my friends, and I do not expect to be one much longer. Indeed, I almost hope not."

"Well, I hope not, too," said the Rat heartily. "You've been a fine bother to us all this time, and I'm glad to hear it's going to stop. And in weather like this, and the boating season just beginning! It's too bad of you, Toad! It isn't the trouble we mind, but you're making us miss such an awful lot."

"I'm afraid it *is* the trouble you mind, though," replied the Toad languidly. "I can quite understand it. It's natural enough. You're tired of bothering about me. I mustn't ask you to do anything further. I'm a nuisance, I know."

"You are, indeed," said the Rat. "But I tell you, I'd take any trouble on earth for you, if only you'd be a sensible animal."

"If I thought that, Ratty," murmured Toad, more feebly than ever, "then I would beg you – for the last time, probably – to step round to the village as quickly as possible – even now it may be too late – and fetch the doctor. But don't you bother. It's only a trouble, and perhaps we may as well let things take their course."

"Why, what do you want a doctor for?" inquired the Rat, coming closer and examining him. He certainly lay very still and flat, and his voice was weaker and his manner much changed.

"Surely you have noticed of late –" murmured Toad. "But no – why should you? Noticing things is only a trouble. To-morrow, indeed, you may be saying to yourself, 'O, if only I had noticed sooner! If only I had done something!' But no; it's a trouble. Never mind – forget that I asked."

"Look here, old man," said the Rat, beginning to get rather alarmed, "of course I'll fetch a doctor to you, if you really think you want him. But you can hardly be bad enough for that yet. Let's talk about something else."

"I fear, dear friend," said Toad, with a sad smile, "that 'talk' can do little in a case like this – or doctors either, for that matter; still, one must grasp at the slightest straw. And, by the way – while you are about it – I *hate* to give you additional trouble, but I happen to remember that you will pass the door – would you mind at the same time asking the lawyer to step up? It would be a convenience to me, and there are moments – perhaps I should say there is *a* moment – when one must face disagreeable tasks, at whatever cost to exhausted nature!"

"A lawyer! O, he must be really bad!" the affrighted Rat said to himself, as he hurried from the room, not forgetting, however, to lock the door carefully behind him.

Outside, he stopped to consider. The other two were far away, and he had no one to consult.

"It's best to be on the safe side," he said, on reflection. "I've known Toad fancy himself frightfully bad before, without the slightest reason; but I've never heard him ask for a lawyer! If there's nothing really the matter, the doctor will tell him he's an old ass, and cheer him up; and that will be something gained. I'd better humour him and go; it won't take very long." So he ran off to the village on his errand of mercy.

The Toad, who had hopped lightly out of bed as soon as he heard the key turned in the lock, watched him eagerly from the window till he disappeared down the carriage-drive. Then, laughing heartily, he dressed as quickly as possible in the smartest suit he could lay hands on at the moment, filled his pockets with cash which he took from a small drawer in the dressing-table, and next, knotting the sheets from his bed together and tying one end of the improvised rope round the central mullion of the handsome Tudor window which formed such a feature of his bedroom, he scrambled out, slid lightly to the ground, and, taking the opposite direction to the Rat, marched off light-heartedly, whistling a merry tune.

It was a gloomy luncheon for Rat when the Badger and the Mole at length returned, and he had to face them at table with his pitiful and unconvincing story. The Badger's caustic, not to say brutal, remarks may be imagined, and therefore passed over; but it was painful to the Rat that even the Mole, though he took his friend's side as far as possible, could not help saying, "You've been a bit of a duffer this time, Ratty! Toad, too, of all animals!"

"He did it awfully well," said the crestfallen Rat.

"He did *you* awfully well!" rejoined the Badger hotly. "However, talking won't mend matters. He's got clear away for the time, that's certain; and the worst of it is, he'll be so conceited with what he'll think is cleverness that he may commit any folly. One comfort is, we're free now, and needn't waste any more of our precious time doing sentry-go. But we'd better continue to sleep at Toad Hall for a while longer. Toad may be brought back at any moment – on a stretcher, or between two policemen."

So spoke the Badger, not knowing what the future held in store, or how much water, and of how turbid a character, was to run under bridges before Toad should sit at ease again in his ancestral Hall.

Meanwhile, Toad, gay and irresponsible, was walking briskly along the high road, some miles from home. At first he had taken by-paths, and crossed many fields, and changed his course several times, in case of pursuit; but now, feeling by this time safe from recapture, and the sun smiling brightly on him, and all Nature joining in a chorus of approval to the song of self-praise that his own heart was singing to him, he almost danced along the road in his satisfaction and conceit.

"Smart piece of work that!" he remarked to himself chuckling. "Brain against brute force – and brain came out on the top – as it's bound to do. Poor old Ratty! My! won't he catch it when the Badger gets back! A worthy fellow, Ratty, with many good qualities, but very little intelligence and absolutely no education. I must take him in hand some day, and see if I can make something of him."

Filled full of conceited thoughts such as these he strode along, his head in the air, till he reached a little town, where the sign of "The Red Lion", swinging across the road halfway down the main street, reminded him that he had not breakfasted that day, and that he was exceedingly hungry after his long walk. He marched into the inn, ordered the best luncheon that could be provided at so short a notice, and sat down to eat it in the coffee-room.

He was about half-way through his meal when an only too familiar sound, approaching down the street, made him start and fall a-trembling all over. The

poop-poop! drew nearer and nearer, the car could be heard to turn into the inn-yard and come to a stop, and Toad had to hold on to the leg of the table to conceal his overmastering emotion. Presently the party entered the coffee-room, hungry, talkative, and gay, voluble on their experiences of the morning and the merits of the chariot that had brought them along so well. Toad listened eagerly, all ears, for a time; at last he could stand it no longer. He slipped out of the room quietly, paid his bill at the bar, and as soon as he got outside sauntered round quietly to the inn-yard. "There cannot be any harm," he said to himself, "in my only just *looking* at it!"

The car stood in the middle of the yard, quite unattended, the stable-helps and other hangers-on being all at their dinner. Toad walked slowly round it, inspecting, criticizing, musing deeply.

"I wonder," he said to himself presently, "I wonder if this sort of car *starts* easily?"

Next moment, hardly knowing how it came about, he found he had hold of the handle and was turning it. As the familiar sound broke forth, the old passion seized on Toad and completely mastered him, body and soul. As if in a dream he found himself, somehow, seated in the driver's seat; as if in a dream, he pulled the lever and swung the car round the yard and out through the archway; and, as if in a dream, all sense of right and wrong, all fear of obvious consequences, seemed temporarily suspended. He increased his pace, and as the car devoured the street and leapt forth on the high road through the open country, he was only conscious that he was Toad once more, Toad at his best and highest, Toad the terror, the traffic-queller, the Lord of the lone trail, before whom all must give way or be smitten into nothingness and everlasting night. He chanted as he flew, and the car responded with sonorous drone; the miles were eaten up under him as he sped he knew not whither, fulfilling his instincts, living his hour, reckless of what might come to him.

"To my mind," observed the Chairman of the Bench of Magistrates cheerfully, "the *only* difficulty that presents itself in this otherwise very clear case is, how we can possibly make it sufficiently hot for the incorrigible rogue and hardened ruffian whom we see cowering in the dock before us. Let me see: he has been found guilty, on the clearest evidence, first, of stealing a valuable motor-car; secondly, of driving to the public danger; and, thirdly, of gross impertinence to the rural police. Mr Clerk, will you tell us, please, what is the very stiffest penalty we can impose for each of these offences? Without, of course, giving the prisoner the benefit of any doubt, because there isn't any."

The Clerk scratched his nose with his pen. "Some people would consider," he observed, "that stealing the motor-car was the worst offence; and so it is. But cheeking the police undoubtedly carries the severest penalty; and so it ought. Supposing you were to say twelve months for the theft, which is mild; and three years for the furious driving, which is lenient; and fifteen years for the cheek, which was pretty bad sort of cheek, judging by what we've heard from the witness-box, even if you only believe one-tenth part of what you heard, and I never believe more myself – those figures, if added together correctly, tot up to nineteen years –"

"First-rate!" said the Chairman.

"– So you had better make it a round twenty years and be on the safe side," concluded the Clerk.

"An excellent suggestion!" said the Chairman approvingly. "Prisoner! Pull yourself together and try and stand up straight. It's going to be twenty years for you this time. And mind, if you appear before us again, upon any charge whatever, we shall have to deal with you very seriously!"

Then the brutal minions of the law fell upon the hapless Toad; loaded him with chains, and dragged him from the Court House, shrieking, praying, protesting; across the market-place, where the playful populace, always as severe upon detected crime as they are sympathetic and helpful when one is merely "wanted", assailed him with jeers, carrots, and popular catch-words; past hooting school-children, their innocent faces lit up with the pleasure they ever derive from the sight of a gentleman in difficulties; across the hollow-

sounding drawbridge, below the spiky portcullis, under the frowning archway of the grim old castle, whose ancient towers soared high overhead; past guardrooms full of grinning soldiery off duty, past sentries who coughed in a horrid sarcastic way, because that is as much as a sentry on his post dare do to show his contempt and abhorrence of crime; up time-worn winding stairs, past men-at-arms in casquet and corselet of steel, darting threatening looks through their vizards; across courtyards, where mastiffs strained at their leash and pawed the air to get at him; past ancient warders, their halberds leant against the wall, dozing over a pasty and a flagon of brown ale; on and on, past the rack-chamber and the thumbscrew-room, past the turning that led to the private scaffold, till they reached the door of the grimmest dungeon that lay in the heart of the innermost keep. There at last they paused, where an ancient gaoler sat fingering a bunch of mighty keys.

"Oddsbodikins!" said the sergeant of police, taking off his helmet and wiping his forehead. "Rouse thee, old loon, and take over from us this vile Toad, a criminal of deepest guilt and matchless artfulness and resource. Watch and ward him with all thy skill; and mark thee well, grey-beard, should aught untoward befall, thy old head shall answer for his – and a murrain on both of them!"

The gaoler nodded grimly, laying his withered hand on the shoulder of the miserable Toad. The rusty key creaked in the lock, the great door clanged behind them; and Toad was a helpless prisoner in the remotest dungeon of the best-guarded keep of the stoutest castle in all the length and breadth of Merry England.

Chapter 7

The Piper at the Gates of Dawn

The Willow-Wren was twittering his thin little song, hidden himself in the dark selvedge of the river bank. Though it was past ten o'clock at night, the sky still clung to and retained some lingering skirts of light from the departed day; and the sullen heats of the torrid afternoon broke up and rolled away at the dispersing touch of the cool fingers of the short midsummer night. Mole lay stretched on the bank, still panting from the stress of the fierce day that had been cloudless from dawn to late sunset, and waited for his friend to return. He had been on the river with some companions, leaving the Water Rat free to keep a engagement of long standing with Otter; and he had come back to find the house dark and deserted, and no sign of Rat, who was doubtless keeping it up late with his old comrade. It was still too hot to think of staying indoors, so he lay on some cool dock-leaves, and thought over the past day and its doings, and how very good they all had been.

The Rat's light footfall was presently heard approaching over the parched grass. "O, the blessed coolness!" he said, and sat down, gazing thoughtfully into the river, silent and preoccupied.

"You stayed to supper, of course?" said the Mole presently.

"Simply had to," said the Rat. "They wouldn't hear of my going before. You know how kind they always are. And they made things as jolly for me as ever they could, right up to the moment I left. But I felt a brute all the time, as it was clear to me they were very unhappy, though they tried to hide it. Mole, I'm afraid they're in trouble. Little Portly is missing again; and you know what a lot his father thinks of him, though he never says much about it."

"What, that child?" said the Mole lightly. "Well, suppose he is; why worry about it? He's always straying off and getting lost, and turning up again; he's so adventurous. But no harm ever happens to him. Everybody hereabouts knows him and likes him, just as they do old Otter, and you may be sure some animal or other will come across him and bring him back again all right. Why, we've found him ourselves, miles from home and quite self-possessed and cheerful!"

"Yes; but this time it's more serious," said the Rat gravely. "He's been missing for some days now, and the Otters have hunted everywhere, high and low, without finding the slightest trace. And they've asked every animal, too, for miles around, and no one knows anything about him. Otter's evidently more anxious than he'll admit. I got out of him that young Portly hasn't learnt to swim very well yet, and I can see he's thinking of the weir. There's a lot of water coming down still, considering the time of year, and the place always had a fascination for the child. And then there are – well, traps and things – *you* know. Otter's not the fellow to be nervous about any son of his before it's time. And now he *is* nervous. When I left, he came out with me – said he wanted some air, and talked about stretching his legs. But I could see it wasn't that, so I drew him out and pumped him, and got it all from him at last. He was going to spend the night watching by the ford. You know the place where the old ford used to be, in bygone days before they built the bridge?"

"I know it well," said the Mole. "But why should Otter choose to watch there?"

"Well, it seems that it was there he gave Portly his first swimming lesson," continued the Rat. "From that shallow, gravelly spit near the bank. And it was there he used to teach him fishing, and there young Portly caught his first fish, of which he was so very proud. The child loved the spot, and Otter thinks that if he came wandering back from wherever he is – if he *is* anywhere by this time, poor little chap – he might make for the ford he was so fond of; or if he came across it he'd remember it well, and stop there and play, perhaps. So Otter goes there every night and watches – on the chance, you know, just on the chance!"

They were silent for a time, both thinking of the same thing – the lonely, heart-sore animal, crouched by the ford, watching and waiting, the long night through – on the chance.

"Well, well," said the Rat presently, "I suppose we ought to be thinking about turning in." But he never offered to move.

"Rat," said the Mole, "I simply can't go and turn in and go to sleep, and *do* nothing, even though there doesn't seem to be anything to be done. We'll get the boat out, and paddle upstream. The moon will be up in an hour or so, and then we will search as well as we can – anyhow, it will be better than going to bed and doing *nothing*."

"Just what I was thinking myself," said the Rat. "It's not the sort of night for bed anyhow; and daybreak is not so very far off, and then we may pick up some news of him from early risers as we go along."

They got the boat out, and the Rat took the sculls, paddling with caution. Out in midstream there was a clear, narrow track that faintly reflected the sky; but wherever shadows fell on the water from bank, bush, or tree, they were as solid to all appearance as the banks themselves, and the Mole had to steer with judgment accordingly. Dark and deserted as it was, the night was full of small noises, song and chatter and rustling, telling of the busy little population who were up and about, plying their trades and vocations through the night till sunshine should fall on them at last and send them off to their well-earned repose. The water's own noises, too, were more apparent than by day, its gurglings and "cloops" more unexpected and near at hand; and constantly they started at what seemed a sudden clear call from an actual articulate voice.

The line of the horizon was clear and hard against the sky, and in one particular quarter it showed black against a silvery climbing phosphorescence that grew and grew. At last, over the rim of the waiting earth the moon lifted with slow majesty till it swung clear of the horizon and rode off, free of moorings; and once more they began to see surfaces – meadows widespread, and quiet gardens; and the river itself from bank to bank, all softly disclosed, all washed clean of mystery and terror, all radiant again as by day, but with a difference that was tremendous. Their old haunts greeted them again in other raiment, as if they had slipped away and put on this pure new apparel and come quietly back, smiling as they shyly waited to see if they would be recognized again under it.

Fastening their boat to a willow, the friends landed in this silent, silver kingdom, and patiently explored the hedges, the hollow trees, the runnels and their little culverts, the ditches and dry waterways. Embarking again and crossing over, they worked their way up the stream in this manner, while the

moon, serene and detached in a cloudless sky, did what she could, though so far off, to help them in their quest; till her hour came and she sank earthwards reluctantly, and left them, and mystery once more held field and river.

Then a change began slowly to declare itself. The horizon became clearer, field and tree came more into sight, and somehow with a different look; the mystery began to drop away from them. A bird piped suddenly, and was still; and a light breeze sprang up and set the reeds and bulrushes rustling. Rat, who was in the stern of the boat, while Mole sculled, sat up suddenly and listened with a passionate intentness. Mole, who with gentle strokes was just keeping the boat moving while he scanned the banks with care, looked at him with curiosity.

"It's gone!" sighed the Rat, sinking back in his seat again. "So beautiful and strange and new! Since it was to end so soon, I almost wish I had never heard it. For it has roused a longing in me that is pain, and nothing seems worth while but just to hear that sound once more and go on listening to it for ever. No! There it is again!" he cried, alert once more. Entranced, he was silent for a long space, spellbound.

"Now it passes on and I begin to lose it," he said presently. "O Mole! the beauty of it! The merry bubble and joy, the thin, clear, happy call of the distant piping! Such music I never dreamed of, and the call in it is stronger even than the music is sweet! Row on, Mole, row! For the music and the call must be for us."

The Mole, greatly wondering, obeyed. "I hear nothing myself," he said, "but the wind playing in the reeds and rushes and osiers."

The Rat never answered, if indeed he heard. Rapt, transported, trembling, he was possessed in all his senses by this new divine thing that caught up his helpless soul and swung and dandled it, a powerless but happy infant, in a strong sustaining grasp.

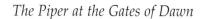

In silence Mole rowed steadily and soon they came to a point where the river divided, a long backwater branching off to one side. With a slight movement of his head, Rat, who had long dropped the rudder-lines, directed the rower to take the backwater. The creeping tide of light gained and gained, and now they could see the colour of the flowers that gemmed the water's edge.

"Clearer and nearer still," cried the Rat joyously. "Now you must surely hear it – Ah – at last – I see you do!"

Breathless and transfixed the Mole stopped rowing as the liquid run of that glad piping broke on him like a wave, caught him up, and possessed him utterly. He saw the tears on his comrade's cheeks, and bowed his head and understood. For a space they hung there, brushed by the purple loosestrife that fringed the bank; then the clear imperious summons that marched hand-in-hand with the intoxicating melody imposed its will on Mole, and mechanically he bent to his oars again. And the light grew steadily stronger, but no birds sang as they were wont to do at the approach of dawn; and but for the heavenly music all was marvellously still.

On either side of them, as they glided onwards, the rich meadow-grass seemed that morning of a freshness and a greenness unsurpassable. Never had they noticed the roses so vivid, the willow-herb so riotous, the meadow-sweet so odorous and pervading. Then the murmur of the approaching weir began to hold the air, and they felt a consciousness that they were nearing the end, whatever it might be, that surely awaited their expedition.

A wide half-circle of foam and glinting lights and shining shoulders of green water, the great weir closed the backwater from bank to bank, troubled all the quiet surface with twirling eddies and floating foam-streaks, and deadened all other sounds with its solemn and soothing rumble. In midmost of the stream, embraced in the weir's shimmering arm-spread, a small island lay anchored, fringed close with willow and silver birch and alder. Reserved, shy, but full of significance, it hid whatever it might hold behind a veil, keeping it till the hour should come, and, with the hour, those who were called and chosen.

Slowly, but with no doubt or hesitation whatever, and in something of a solemn expectancy, the two animals passed through the broken tumultuous water and moored their boat at the flowery margin of the island. In silence they landed, and pushed through the blossom and scented herbage and undergrowth that led up to the level ground, till they stood on a little lawn of a marvellous green, set round with Nature's own orchard-trees – crab-apple, wild cherry, and sloe.

"This is the place of my song-dream, the place the music played to me," whispered the Rat, as if in a trance. "Here, in this holy place, here if anywhere, surely we shall find Him!"

Then suddenly the Mole felt a great Awe fall upon him, an awe that turned his muscles to water, bowed his head, and rooted his feet to the ground. It was no panic terror – indeed he felt wonderfully at peace and happy – but it was an awe that smote and held him and, without seeing, he knew it could only mean that some august Presence was very, very near. With difficulty he turned to look for his friend, and saw him at his side, cowed, stricken, and trembling violently. And still there was utter silence in the populous bird-haunted branches around them; and still the light grew and grew.

Perhaps he would never have dared to raise his eyes, but that, though the piping was now hushed, the call and the summons seemed still dominant and imperious. He might not refuse, were Death himself waiting to strike him instantly, once he had looked with mortal eye on things rightly kept hidden. Trembling he obeyed, and raised his humble head; and then, in that utter clearness of the imminent dawn, while Nature, flushed with fullness of incredible colour, seemed to hold her breath for the event, he looked in the very eyes of the Friend and Helper; saw the backward sweep of the curved horns, gleaming in the growing daylight; saw the stern, hooked nose between the kindly eyes that were looking down on them humorously, while the bearded mouth broke into a half-smile at the corners; saw the rippling muscles on the arm that lay across the broad chest, the long supple hand still holding the pan-pipes only just fallen away from the parted lips; saw the splendid curves of the shaggy limbs disposed in majestic ease on the sward; saw, last of all, nestling between his very hooves, sleeping soundly in entire peace and contentment, the little, round, podgy, childish form of the baby otter. All this he saw, for one moment breathless and intense, vivid on the morning sky; and still, as he looked, he lived; and still, as he lived, he wondered.

"Rat!" he found breath to whisper, shaking. "Are you afraid?"

"Afraid?" murmured the Rat, his eyes shining with unutterable love. "Afraid! Of *Him*? O, never, never! And yet – and yet – O, Mole, I am afraid!"

Then the two animals, crouching to the earth, bowed their heads and did worship.

Sudden and magnificent, the sun's broad golden disc showed itself over the horizon facing them; and the first rays, shooting across the level water-meadows, took the animals full in the eyes and dazzled them. When they were able to look once more, the Vision had vanished, and the air was full of the carol of birds that hailed the dawn.

As they stared blankly, in dumb misery deepening as they slowly realized all they had seen and all they had lost, a capricious little breeze, dancing up from the surface of the water, tossed the aspens, shook the dewy roses, and blew lightly and caressingly in their faces, and with its soft touch came instant oblivion. For this is the last best gift that the kindly demigod is careful to bestow on those to whom he has revealed himself in their helping: the gift of forgetfulness. Lest the awful remembrance should remain and grow, and overshadow mirth and pleasure, and the great haunting memory should spoil all the after-lives of little animals helped out of difficulties, in order that they should be happy and light-hearted as before.

Mole rubbed his eyes and stared at Rat, who was looking about him in a puzzled sort of way. "I beg your pardon; what did you say, Rat?" he asked.

"I think I was only remarking," said Rat slowly, "that this was the right sort of place and that here, if anywhere, we should find him. And look! Why, there he is, the little fellow!" And with a cry of delight he ran towards the slumbering Portly.

But Mole stood still a moment, held in thought. As one wakened suddenly from a beautiful dream, who struggles to recall it, and can recapture nothing but a dim sense of the beauty of it, the beauty! Till that, too, fades away in its turn, and the dreamer bitterly accepts the hard, cold waking and all its penalties; so Mole, after struggling with his memory for a

brief space, shook his head sadly and followed the Rat.

Portly woke up with a joyous squeak, and wriggled with pleasure at the sight of his father's friends, who had played with him so often in past days. In a moment, however, his face grew blank, and he fell to hunting round in a circle with pleading whine. As a child that has fallen happily asleep in its nurse's arms, and wakes to find itself alone and laid in a strange place, and searches corners and cupboards, and runs from room to room, despair growing silently in its heart, even so Portly searched the island and searched, dogged and unwearying, till at last the black moment came for giving it up and sitting down and crying bitterly.

The Mole ran quickly to comfort the little animal; but Rat, lingering, looked long and doubtfully at certain hoof-marks deep in the sward.

"Some – great – animal – has been here," he murmured slowly and thoughtfully; and stood musing, musing; his mind strangely stirred.

"Come along, Rat!" called the Mole. "Think of poor Otter, waiting up there by the ford!"

Portly had soon been comforted by the promise of a treat – a jaunt on the river in Mr Rat's real boat; and the two animals conducted him to the water's side, placed him securely between them in the bottom of the boat, and paddled off down the backwater. The sun was fully up by now, and hot on them, birds sang lustily and without restraint, and flowers smiled and nodded from either bank, but somehow – so thought the animals – with less of richness and blaze of colour than they seemed to remember seeing quite recently somewhere – they wondered where.

The main river reached again, they turned the boat's head upstream, towards the point

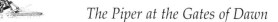

where they knew their friend was keeping his lonely vigil. As they drew near the familiar ford, the Mole took the boat in to the bank, and they lifted Portly out and set him on his legs on the tow-path, gave him his marching orders and a friendly farewell pat on the back, and shoved out into midstream. They watched the little animal as he waddled along the path contentedly and with importance; watched him till they saw his muzzle suddenly lift and his waddle break into a clumsy amble as he quickened his pace with shrill whines and wriggles of recognition. Looking up the river, they could see Otter start up, tense and rigid, from out of the shallows where he crouched in dumb patience,

and could hear his amazed and joyous bark as he bounded up through the osiers on to the path. Then the Mole, with a strong pull on one oar, swung the boat round and let the full stream bear them down again whither it would, their quest now happily ended.

"I feel strangely tired, Rat," said the Mole, leaning wearily over his oars as the boat drifted. "It's being up all night, you'll say, perhaps; but that's nothing. We do as much half the nights of the week, at this time of the year. No; I feel as if I had been through something very exciting and rather terrible, and it was just over; and yet nothing particular has happened."

"Or something very surprising and splendid and beautiful," murmured the Rat, leaning back and closing his eyes. "I feel just as you do, Mole; simply dead tired, though not body tired. It's lucky we've got the stream with us, to take us home. Isn't it jolly to feel the sun again, soaking into one's bones! And hark to the wind playing in the reeds!"

"It's like music – far-away music," said the Mole, nodding drowsily.

"So I was thinking," murmured the Rat, dreamful and languid. "Dance-music – the lilting sort that runs on without a stop – but with words in it, too – it passes into words and out of them again – I catch them at intervals – then it is dance-music once more, and then nothing but the reeds' soft thin whispering."

"You hear better than I," said the Mole sadly. "I cannot catch the words."

"Let me try and give you them," said the Rat softly, his eyes still closed. "Now it is turning into words again – faint but clear – *Lest the awe should dwell – And turn your frolic to fret – You shall look on my power at the helping hour – But then you shall forget!* Now the reeds take it up – *forget, forget,* they sigh, and it dies away in a rustle and a whisper. Then the voice returns –

"*Lest limbs be reddened and rent – I spring the trap that is set – As I loose the snare you may glimpse me there – For surely you shall forget!* Row nearer, Mole, nearer to the reeds! It is hard to catch, and grows each minute fainter.

"*Helper and healer, I cheer – Small waifs in the woodland wet – Strays I find in it, wounds I bind in it – Bidding them all forget!* Nearer, Mole, nearer! No, it is no good; the song has died away into reed-talk."

"But what do the words mean?" asked the wondering Mole.

"That I do not know," said the Rat simply. "I passed them on to you as they reached me. Ah! now they return again, and this time full and clear! This time, at last, it is the real, the unmistakable thing, simple – passionate – perfect –"

"Well, let's have it, then," said the Mole, after he had waited patiently for a few minutes, half dozing in the hot sun.

But no answer came. He looked, and understood the silence. With a smile of much happiness on his face, and something of a listening look still lingering there, the weary Rat was fast asleep.

Chapter 8

Toad's Adventures

When Toad found himself immured in a dank and noisome dungeon, and knew that all the grim darkness of a medieval fortress lay between him and the outer world of sunshine and well-metalled high roads where he had lately been so happy, disporting himself as if he had bought up every road in England, he flung himself at full length on the floor, and shed bitter tears, and abandoned himself to dark despair. "This is the end of everything" (he said), "at least it is the end of the career of Toad, which is the same thing; the popular and handsome Toad, the rich and hospitable Toad, the Toad so free and careless and debonair! How can I hope to be ever set at large again" (he said), "who have been imprisoned so justly for stealing so handsome a motor-car in such an audacious manner, and for such lurid and imaginative cheek, bestowed upon such a number of fat, red-faced policemen!" (Here his sobs choked him.) "Stupid animal that I was" (he said), "now I must languish in this dungeon, till people who were proud to say they knew me, have forgotten the very name of Toad! O wise old Badger!" (he said), "O clever, intelligent Rat and sensible Mole! What sound judgments, what a knowledge of men and matters you possess! O unhappy and forsaken Toad!" With lamentations such as these he passed his days and nights for several weeks, refusing his meals or intermediate light refreshments, though the grim and ancient gaoler, knowing that Toad's pockets were well lined, frequently pointed out that many comforts, and indeed luxuries, could by arrangement be sent in – at a price – from outside.

Now the gaoler had a daughter, a pleasant wench and good-hearted, who assisted her father in the lighter duties of his post. She was particularly fond of animals, and, besides her canary, whose cage hung on a nail in the massive wall of the keep by day, to the great annoyance of prisoners who relished an after-dinner nap, and was shrouded in an antimacassar on the parlour table at night, she kept several piebald mice and a restless revolving squirrel. This kind-hearted girl, pitying the misery of Toad, said to her father one day, "Father! I can't bear to see that poor beast so unhappy, and getting so thin! You let me have the managing of him. You know how fond of animals I am. I'll make him eat from my hand, and sit up, and do all sorts of things."

Her father replied that she could do what she liked with him. He was tired of Toad, and his sulks and his airs and his meanness. So that day she went on her errand of mercy, and knocked at the door of Toad's cell.

"Now, cheer up, Toad," she said, coaxingly, on entering, "and sit up and dry your eyes and be a sensible animal. And do try and eat a bit of dinner. See, I've brought you some of mine, hot from the oven!"

It was bubble-and-squeak, between two plates, and its fragrance filled the narrow cell. The penetrating smell of cabbage reached the nose of Toad as he lay prostrate in his misery on the floor, and gave him the idea for a moment that perhaps life was not such a blank and desperate thing as he had imagined. But still he wailed, and kicked with his legs, and refused to be comforted. So the wise girl retired for the time, but, of course, a good deal of the smell of hot cabbage remained behind, as it will do, and Toad, between his sobs, sniffed and reflected, and gradually began to think new and inspiring thoughts: of chivalry, and poetry, and deeds still to be done; of broad meadows, and cattle browsing in them, raked by sun and wind; of kitchen-gardens, and straight herb-borders, and warm snap-dragon beset by bees; and of the comforting clink of dishes set down on the table at Toad Hall, and the scrape of chair-legs on the floor as everyone pulled himself close up to his work. The air of the narrow cell took on a rosy tinge; he began to think of his friends, and how they would surely be able to do something; of lawyers, and how they would have enjoyed his case, and what an ass he had been not to get in a few; and lastly, he thought of his own great cleverness and resource, and all that he was capable of if he only gave his great mind to it; and the cure was almost complete.

When the girl returned, some hours later, she carried a tray, with a cup of fragrant tea steaming on it; and a plate piled up with very hot buttered toast, cut thick, very brown on both sides, with the butter running through the holes in it in great golden drops, like honey from the honeycomb. The smell of that buttered toast simply talked to Toad, and with no uncertain voice; talked of warm kitchens, of breakfasts on bright frosty mornings, of cosy parlour firesides on winter evenings, when one's ramble was over and slippered feet were propped on the fender; of the purring of contented cats, and the twitter of sleepy canaries. Toad sat up on end once more, dried his eyes, sipped his tea and munched his toast, and soon began talking freely about himself, and the house he lived in, and his doings there, and how important he was, and what a lot his friends thought of him.

The gaoler's daughter saw that the topic was doing him as much good as the tea, as indeed it was, and encouraged him to go on.

"Tell me about Toad Hall," said she. "It sounds beautiful."

"Toad Hall," said the Toad proudly, "is an eligible self-contained gentle-man's residence very unique; dating in part from the fourteenth century, but replete with every modern convenience. Up-to-date sanitation. Five minutes from church, post-office, and golf-links, Suitable for –"

"Bless the animal," said the girl, laughing, "I don't want to *take* it. Tell me something *real* about it. But first wait till I fetch you some more tea and toast."

She tripped away, and presently returned with a fresh trayful; and Toad, pitching into the toast with avidity, his spirits quite restored to their usual level, told her about the boathouse, and the fish-pond, and the old walled

kitchen-garden; and about the pig-styes, and the stables,
and the pigeon-house, and the hen-house; and about the
dairy, and the wash-house, and the china-cupboards,
and the linen-presses (she liked that bit especially);
and about the banqueting-hall, and the fun
they had there when the other
animals were
gathered round the
table and Toad was
at his best,
singing songs,
telling stories,
carrying on generally.
Then she wanted to
know about his animal-friends,
and was very interested in all he had to
tell her about them and how they lived, and what they
did to pass their time. Of course, she did not say she was fond of animals as *pets*,
because she had the sense to see that Toad would be extremely offended. When
she said good night, having filled his water-jug and shaken up his straw for him,
Toad was very much the same sanguine, self-satisfied animal that he had been of
old. He sang a little song or two, of the sort he used to sing at his dinner-parties,
curled himself up in the straw, and had an excellent night's rest and the
pleasantest of dreams.

They had many interesting talks together, after that, as the dreary days went
on; and the gaoler's daughter grew very sorry for Toad, and thought it a great
shame that a poor little animal should be locked up in prison for what seemed
to her a very trivial offence. Toad, of course, in his vanity, thought that her

interest in him proceeded from a growing tenderness; and he could not help half regretting that the social gulf between them was so very wide, for she was a comely lass, and evidently admired him very much.

One morning the girl was very thoughtful, and answered at random, and did not seem to Toad to be paying proper attention to his witty sayings and sparkling comments.

"Toad," she said presently, "just listen, please. I have an aunt who is a washerwoman."

"There, there," said Toad, graciously and affably, "never mind; think no more about it. *I* have several aunts who *ought* to be washerwomen."

"Do be quiet a minute, Toad," said the girl. "You talk too much, that's your chief fault, and I'm trying to think, and you hurt my head. As I said, I have an aunt who is a washerwoman; she does the washing for all the prisoners in this castle – we try to keep any paying business of that sort in the family, you understand. She takes out the washing on Monday morning, and brings it in on Friday evening. This is a Thursday. Now, this is what occurs to me: you're very rich – at least you're always telling me so – and she's very poor. A few pounds wouldn't make any difference to you, and it would mean a lot to her. Now, I think if she were properly approached – squared, I believe is the word you animals use – you could come to some arrangement by which she would let you have her dress and bonnet and so on, and you could escape from the castle as the official washerwoman. You're very alike in many respects – particularly about the figure."

"We're *not*," said the Toad in a huff. "I have a very elegant figure – for what I am."

"So has my aunt," replied the girl, "for what *she* is. But have it your own way. You horrid, proud, ungrateful animal, when I'm sorry for you, and trying to help you!"

"Yes, yes, that's all right; thank you very much indeed," said the Toad hurriedly. "'But look here! you wouldn't surely have Mr Toad of Toad Hall, going about the country disguised as a washerwoman!"

"Then you can stop here as a Toad," replied the girl with much spirit. "I suppose you want to go off in a coach-and-four!"

Honest Toad was always ready to admit himself in the wrong. "You are a good, kind, clever girl," he said, "and I am indeed a proud and a stupid toad. Introduce me to your worthy aunt, if you will be so kind, and I have no doubt that the excellent lady and I will be able to arrange terms satisfactory to both parties."

Next evening the girl ushered her aunt into Toad's cell, bearing his week's washing pinned up in a towel. The old lady had been prepared beforehand for the interview, and the sight of certain gold sovereigns that Toad had thoughtfully placed on the table in full view practically completed the matter and left little further to discuss. In return for his cash, Toad received a cotton print gown, an apron, a shawl, and a rusty black bonnet; the only stipulation the old lady made being that she should be gagged and bound and dumped down in a corner. By this not very convincing artifice, she explained, aided by picturesque fiction which she could supply herself, she hoped to retain her situation, in spite of the suspicious appearance of things.

Toad was delighted with the suggestion. It would enable him to leave the prison in some style, and with his reputation for being a desperate and dangerous fellow untarnished; and he readily helped the gaoler's daughter to make her aunt appear as much as possible the victim of circumstances over which she had no control.

"Now it's your turn, Toad," said the girl. "Take off that coat and waistcoat of yours; you're fat enough as it is."

Shaking with laughter, she proceeded to "hook-and-eye" him into the cotton print gown, arranged the shawl with a professional fold, and tied the strings of the rusty bonnet under his chin.

"You're the very image of her," she giggled, "only I'm sure you never looked half so respectable in all your life before. Now, good-bye, Toad, and good luck.

Go straight down the way you came up; and if anyone says anything to you, as they probably will, being but men, you can chaff back a bit, of course, but remember you're a widow woman, quite alone in the world, with a character to lose."

With a quaking heart, but as firm a footstep as he could command, Toad set forth cautiously on what seemed to be a most hare-brained and hazardous undertaking; but he was soon agreeably surprised to find how easy everything was made for him, and a little humbled at the thought that both his popularity, and the sex that seemed to inspire it, were really another's. The washerwoman's squat figure in its familiar cotton print seemed a passport for every barred door and grim gateway; even when he hesitated, uncertain as to the right turning to take, he found himself helped out of his difficulty by the warder at the next gate, anxious to be off to his tea, summoning him to come along sharp and not keep him waiting there all night. The chaff and the humorous sallies to which he was subjected, and to which, of course, he had to provide prompt and effective reply, formed, indeed, his chief danger; for Toad was an animal with a strong sense of his own dignity, and the chaff was mostly (he thought) poor and clumsy, and the humour of the sallies entirely lacking.

However, he kept his temper, though with great difficulty, suited his retorts to his company and his supposed character, and did his best not to overstep the limits of good taste.

It seemed hours before he crossed the last courtyard, rejected the pressing invitations from the last guardroom, and dodged the outspread arms of the last warder, pleading with simulated passion for just one farewell embrace. But at last he heard the wicket-gate in the great outer door click behind him, felt the fresh air of the outer world upon his anxious brow, and knew that he was free!

Dizzy with the easy success of his daring exploit, he walked quickly towards the lights of the town, not knowing in the least what he should do next, only quite certain of one thing, that he must remove himself as quickly as possible from the neighbourhood where the lady he was forced to represent was so well-known and so popular a character.

As he walked along, considering, his attention was caught by some red and green lights a little way off, to one side of the town, and the sound of the puffing and snorting of engines and the banging of shunted trucks fell on his ear. "Aha!" he thought, "this is a piece of luck! A railway station is the thing I want most in the whole world at this moment; and what's more, I needn't go through the town to get it, and shan't have to support this humiliating character by repartees which, though thoroughly effective, do not assist one's sense of self-respect."

He made his way to the station accordingly, consulted a time-table, and found that a train, bound more or less in the direction of his home, was due to

start in half-an-hour. "More luck!" said Toad, his spirits rising rapidly, and went off to the booking-office to buy his ticket.

He gave the name of the station that he knew to be nearest to the village of which Toad Hall was the principal feature, and mechanically put his fingers, in search of the necessary money, where his waistcoat pocket should have been. But here the cotton gown, which had nobly stood by him so far, and which he had basely forgotten, intervened, and frustrated his efforts. In a sort of nightmare he struggled with the strange uncanny thing that seemed to hold his hands, turn all muscular strivings to water, and laugh at him all the time; while other travellers, forming up in a line behind, waited with impatience, making suggestions of more or less value and comments of more or less stringency and point. At last – somehow – he never rightly understood how – he burst the barriers, attained the goal, arrived at where all waistcoat pockets are eternally situated, and found – not only no money, but no pocket to hold it, and no waistcoat to hold the pocket!

To his horror he recollected that he had left both coat and waistcoat behind him in his cell, and with them his pocket-book, money, keys, watch, matches, pencil-case – all that makes life worth living, all that distinguishes the many-pocketed animal, the lord of creation, from the inferior one-pocketed or no-pocketed productions that hop or trip about permissively, unequipped for the real contest.

In his misery he made one desperate effort to carry the thing off, and, with a return to his fine old manner – a blend of the Squire and the College Don – he said, "Look here! I find I've left my purse behind. Just give me that ticket, will you, and I'll send the money on to-morrow? I'm well-known in these parts."

The clerk stared at him and the rusty black bonnet a moment, and then laughed. "I should think you were pretty well-known in these parts," he said, "if you've tried this game on often. Here, stand away from the window, please, madam; you're obstructing the other passengers!"

An old gentleman who had been prodding him in the back for some moments here thrust him away, and, what was worse, addressed him as his good woman, which angered Toad more than anything that had occurred that evening.

Baffled and full of despair, he wandered blindly down the platform where the train was standing, and tears trickled down each side of his nose. It was hard, he thought, to be within sight of safety and almost of home, and to be baulked by the want of a few wretched shillings and by the pettifogging mistrustfulness of paid officials. Very soon his escape would be discovered, the hunt would be up, he would be caught, reviled, loaded with chains, dragged back again to prison and bread-and-water and straw; his guards and penalties would be doubled; and O, what sarcastic remarks the girl would make! What was to be done? He was not swift of foot; his figure was unfortunately recognizable. Could he not squeeze under the seat of a carriage? He had seen this method adopted by schoolboys, when the journey-money provided by thoughtful parents had been diverted to other and better ends. As he pondered, he found himself opposite the engine, which was being oiled, wiped, and generally caressed by its affectionate driver, a burly man with an oil-can in one hand and a lump of cotton-waste in the other.

"Hullo, mother!" said the engine-driver, "what's the trouble? You don't look particularly cheerful."

"O, sir!" said Toad, crying afresh, "I am a poor unhappy washerwoman, and I've lost all my money, and can't pay for a ticket, and I *must* get home to-night somehow, and whatever I am to do I don't know. O dear, O dear!"

"That's a bad business, indeed," said the engine-driver reflectively. "Lost your money – and can't get home – and got some kids, too, waiting for you, I dare say?"

"Any amount of 'em," sobbed Toad. "And they'll be hungry – and playing with matches – and upsetting lamps, the little innocents! – and quarrelling, and going on generally. O dear, O dear!"

"Well, I'll tell you what I'll do," said the good engine-driver. "You're a washerwoman to your trade, says you. Very well, that's that. And I'm an engine-driver, as you well may see, and there's no denying it's terribly dirty work. Uses up a power of shirts, it does, till my missus is fair tired of washing of 'em. If you'll wash a few shirts for me when you get home, and send 'em along, I'll give you a ride on my engine. It's against the Company's regulations, but we're not so very particular in these out-of-the-way parts."

The Toad's misery turned into rapture as he eagerly scrambled up into the cab of the engine. Of course, he had never washed a shirt in his life, and couldn't if he tried and, anyhow, he wasn't going to begin; but he thought: "When I get safely home to Toad Hall, and have money again, and pockets to put it in, I will send the engine-driver enough to pay for quite a quantity of washing, and that will be the same thing, or better."

The guard waved his welcome flag, the engine-driver whistled in cheerful response, and the train moved out of the station. As the speed increased, and the Toad could see on either side of him real fields, and trees, and hedges, and cows, and horses, all flying past him, and as he thought how every minute was bringing him nearer to Toad Hall, and sympathetic friends, and money to chink in his pocket, and a soft bed to sleep in, and good things to eat, and praise and admiration at the recital of his adventures and his surpassing cleverness, he began to skip up and down and shout and sing snatches of song, to the great astonishment of the engine-driver, who had come across washerwomen before, at long intervals, but never one at all like this.

They had covered many and many a mile, and Toad was already considering what he would have for supper as soon as he got home, when he noticed that the engine-driver, with a puzzled expression on his face, was leaning over the side of the engine and listening hard. Then he saw him climb on to the coals and gaze out over the top of the train; then he returned and said to Toad: "It's very strange; we're the last train running in this direction to-night, yet I could be sworn that I heard another following us!"

Toad ceased his frivolous antics at once. He became grave and depressed, and a dull pain in the lower part of his spine, communicating itself to his legs, made him want to sit down and try desperately not to think of all the possibilities.

By this time the moon was shining brightly, and the engine-driver, steadying himself on the coal, could command a view of the line behind them for a long distance.

Presently he called out, "I can see it clearly now! It is an engine, on our rails, coming along at a great pace! It looks as if we were being pursued!"

The miserable Toad, crouching in the coal-dust, tried hard to think of something to do, with dismal want of success.

"They are gaining on us fast!" cried the engine-driver. "And the engine is crowded with the queerest lot of people! Men like ancient warders, waving halberds; policemen in their helmets, waving truncheons; and shabbily-dressed men in pot-hats, obvious and unmistakable plain-clothes detectives even at this distance, waving revolvers and walking-sticks; all waving, and all shouting the same thing – 'Stop, stop, stop!'"

Then Toad fell on his knees among the coals and, raising his clasped paws in supplication, cried, "Save me, only save me, dear kind Mr Engine-driver, and I will confess everything! I am not the simple washerwoman I seem to be! I

have no children waiting for me, innocent or otherwise! I am a toad – the well-known and popular Mr Toad, a landed proprietor; I have just escaped, by my great daring and cleverness, from a loathsome dungeon into which my enemies had flung me; and if those fellows on that engine recapture me, it will be chains and bread-and-water and straw and misery once more for poor, unhappy, innocent Toad!"

The engine-driver looked down upon him very sternly, and said, "Now tell the truth; what were you put in prison for?"

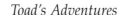

"It was nothing very much," said poor Toad, colouring deeply. "I only borrowed a motor-car while the owners were at lunch; they had no need of it at the time. I didn't mean to steal it, really; but people – especially magistrates – take such harsh views of thoughtless and high-spirited actions."

The engine-driver looked very grave and said, "I fear that you have been indeed a wicked toad, and by rights I ought to give you up to offended justice. But you are evidently in sore trouble and distress, so I will not desert you. I don't hold with motor-cars, for one thing; and I don't hold with being ordered about by policemen when I'm on my own engine, for another. And the sight of an animal in tears always makes me feel queer and soft-hearted. So cheer up, Toad! I'll do my best, and we may beat them yet!"

They piled on more coals, shovelling furiously; the furnace roared, the sparks flew, the engine leapt and swung but still their pursuers slowly gained. The engine-driver, with a sigh, wiped his brow with a handful of cotton-waste, and said, "I'm afraid it's no good, Toad. You see, they are running light, and they have the better engine. There's just one thing left for us to do, and it's your only chance, so attend very carefully to what I tell you. A short way ahead of us is a long tunnel, and on the other side of that the line passes through a thick wood. Now, I will put on all the speed I can while we are running through the tunnel, but the other fellows will slow down a bit, naturally, for fear of an accident. When we are through, I will shut off steam and put on brakes as hard as I can, and the moment it's safe to do so you must jump and hide in the wood, before they get through the tunnel and see you. Then I will go full speed ahead again, and they can chase *me* if they like, for as long as they like, and as far as they like. Now mind and be ready to jump when I tell you!"

They piled on more coals, and the train shot into the tunnel, and the engine rushed and roared and rattled, till at last they shot out at the other end into fresh air and the peaceful moonlight, and saw the wood lying dark and helpful upon either side of the line. The driver shut off steam and put on brakes, the Toad got down on the step, and as the train slowed down to almost a walking pace he heard the driver call out, "Now, jump!"

Toad jumped, rolled down a short embankment, picked himself up unhurt, scrambled into the wood and hid.

Peeping out, he saw his train get up speed again and disappear at a great pace. Then out of the tunnel burst the pursuing engine, roaring and whistling, her motley crew waving their various weapons and shouting, "Stop! stop! stop!" When they were past, the Toad had a hearty laugh – for the first time since he was thrown into prison.

But he soon stopped laughing when he came to consider that it was now very late and dark and cold, and he was in an unknown wood, with no money and no chance of supper, and still far from friends and home; and the dead silence of everything, after the roar and rattle of the train, was something of a shock. He dared not leave the shelter of the trees, so he struck into the wood, with the idea of leaving the railway as far as possible behind him.

After so many weeks within walls, he found the wood strange and unfriendly and inclined, he thought, to make fun of him. Night-jars, sounding their mechanical rattle, made him think that the wood was full of searching warders, closing in on him. An owl, swooping noiselessly towards him, brushed his shoulder with its wing, making him jump with the horrid certainty that it was a hand; then flitted off, moth-like, laughing its low ho! ho! ho! which Toad thought in very poor taste. Once he met a fox, who stopped, looked him up and down in a sarcastic sort of way, and said, "Hullo, washerwoman! Half a pair of socks and a pillow-case short this week! Mind it doesn't occur again!" and swaggered off, sniggering.

Toad looked about for a stone to throw at him, but could not succeed in finding one, which vexed him more than anything. At last, cold, hungry, and

tired out, he sought the shelter of a hollow tree, where with branches and dead leaves he made himself as comfortable a bed as he could, and slept soundly till the morning.

Chapter 9

Wayfarers All

The Water Rat was restless, and he did not exactly know why. To all appearance the summer's pomp was still at fullest height, and although in the tilled acres green had given way to gold, though rowans were reddening, and the woods were dashed here and there with a tawny fierceness, yet light and warmth and colour were still present in undiminished measure, clean of any chilly premonitions of the passing year. But the constant chorus of the orchards and hedges had shrunk to a casual evensong from a few yet unwearied performers; the robin was beginning to assert himself once more; and there was a feeling in the air of change and departure. The cuckoo, of course, had long been silent; but many another feathered friend, for months a part of the familiar landscape and its small society, was missing too and it seemed that the ranks thinned steadily day by day. Rat, ever observant of all winged movement, saw that it was taking daily a southing tendency; and even as he lay in bed at night he thought he could make out, passing in the darkness overhead, the beat and quiver of impatient pinions, obedient to the peremptory call.

Nature's Grand Hotel has its Season, like the others. As the guests one by one pack, pay, and depart, and the seats at the *table-d'hôte* shrink pitifully at each succeeding meal; as suites of rooms are closed, carpets taken up, and waiters sent away; those boarders who are staying on, *en pension*, until the next year's full re-opening, cannot help being somewhat affected by all these flittings and farewells, this eager discussion of plans, routes, and fresh quarters, this daily shrinkage in the stream of comradeship. One gets unsettled, depressed, and inclined to be querulous. Why this craving for change? Why not stay on quietly here, like us, and be jolly? You don't know this hotel out of the season, and what fun we have among ourselves, we fellows who remain and see the whole interesting year out. All very true, no doubt the others always reply; we quite envy you – and some other year perhaps – but just now we have engagements – and there's the bus at the door – our time is up! So they depart, with a smile and a nod, and we miss them, and feel resentful. The Rat was a self-sufficing sort of animal, rooted to the land, and, whoever went, he stayed; still, he could not help noticing what was in the air, and feeling some of its influence in his bones.

It was difficult to settle down to anything seriously, with all this flitting going on. Leaving the water-side, where rushes stood thick and tall in a stream that was becoming sluggish and low, he wandered country-wards, crossed a field or two of pasturage already looking dusty and parched, and thrust into the great realm of wheat, yellow, wavy, and murmurous, full of quiet motion and small whisperings. Here he often loved to wander, through the forest of stiff strong stalks that carried their own golden sky away over his head – a sky that was always dancing, shimmering, softly talking; or swaying strongly to the passing wind and recovering itself with a toss and a merry laugh. Here, too, he had many small friends, a society complete in itself, leading full and busy lives, but always with a spare moment to gossip, and exchange news with a visitor. Today, however, though they were civil enough, the field-mice and harvest-mice seemed preoccupied. Many were digging and tunnelling busily; others, gathered together in small groups, examined plans and drawings of small flats, stated to be desirable and compact, and situated conveniently near the Stores. Some were hauling out dusty trunks and dress-baskets, others were already elbow-deep packing their belongings; while everywhere piles and bundles of wheat, oats, barley, beech-mast and nuts, lay about ready for transport.

"Here's old Ratty!" they cried as soon as they saw him. "Come and bear a hand, Rat, and don't stand about idle!"

"What sort of games are you up to?" said the Water Rat severely. "You know it isn't time to be thinking of winter quarters yet, by a long way!"

"O yes, we know that," explained a field-mouse rather shamefacedly; "but it's always as well to be in good time, isn't it? We really *must* get all the furniture and baggage and stores moved out of this before those horrid machines begin clicking round the fields; and then, you know, the best flats get picked up so quickly nowadays, and if you're late you have to put up with *anything*; and they want such a lot of doing up, too, before they're fit to move into. Of course, we're early, we know that; but we're only just making a start."

"O, bother *starts*," said the Rat. "It's a splendid day. Come for a row, or a stroll along the hedges, or a picnic in the woods, or something."

"Well, I *think* not *to-day*, thank you," replied the field-mouse hurriedly. "Perhaps some *other* day – when we've more *time* –"

The Rat, with a snort of contempt, swung round to go, tripped over a hat-box, and fell, with undignified remarks.

"If people would be more careful," said a field-mouse rather stiffly, "and look where they're going, people wouldn't hurt themselves – and forget themselves. Mind that hold-all, Rat! You'd better sit down somewhere. In an hour or two we may be more free to attend to you."

"You won't be 'free' as you call it much this side of Christmas, I can see that," retorted the Rat grumpily, as he picked his way out of the field.

He returned somewhat despondently to his river again – his faithful, steady-going old river, which never packed up, flitted, or went into winter quarters.

In the osiers which fringed the bank he spied a swallow sitting. Presently it was joined by another, and then by a third; and the birds, fidgeting restlessly on their bough, talked together earnestly and low.

"What, *already?*" said the Rat, strolling up to them. "What's the hurry? I call it simply ridiculous."

"O, we're not off yet, if that's what you mean," replied the first swallow. "We're only making plans and arranging things. Talking it over, you know – what route we're taking this year, and where we'll stop, and so on. That's half the fun!"

"Fun?" said the Rat; "now that's just what I don't understand. If you've *got* to leave this pleasant place, and your friends who will miss you, and your snug homes that you've just settled into, why, when the hour strikes I've no doubt you'll go bravely, and face all the trouble and discomfort and change and newness, and make believe that you're not very unhappy. But to want to talk about it, or even think about it, till you really need –"

"No, you don't understand, naturally," said the second swallow. "First, we feel it stirring within us, a sweet unrest; then back come the recollections one by one, like homing pigeons. They flutter through our dreams at night, they fly with us in our wheelings and circlings by day. We hunger to inquire of each other, to compare notes and assure ourselves that it was all really true, as one by one the scents and sounds and names of long-forgotten places come gradually back and beckon to us."

"Couldn't you stop on for just this year?" suggested the Water Rat, wistfully. "We'll all do our best to make you feel at home. You've no idea what good times we have here, while you are far away."

"I tried 'stopping on' one year," said the third swallow. "I had grown so fond of the place that when the time came I hung back and let the others go on without me. For a few weeks it was all well enough, but afterwards, O the weary length of the nights! The shivering, sunless days! The air so clammy and chill, and not an insect in an acre of it! No, it was no good; my courage broke down, and one cold, stormy night I took wing, flying well inland on account of the strong easterly gales. It was snowing hard as I beat through the passes of the great mountains, and I had a stiff fight to win through; but never shall I forget the blissful feeling of the hot sun again on my back as I sped down to the lakes that lay so blue and placid below me, and the taste of my first fat insect! The past was like a bad dream; the future was all happy holiday as I moved Southwards week by week, easily, lazily, lingering as long as I dared, but always heeding the call! No, I had

had my warning; never again did I think of disobedience."

"Ah, yes, the call of the South, of the South!" twittered the other two dreamily. "Its songs, its hues, its radiant air! O, do you remember –" and, forgetting the Rat, they slid into passionate reminiscence, while he listened fascinated, and his heart burned within him. In himself, too, he knew that it was vibrating at last, that chord hitherto dormant and unsuspected. The mere chatter of these southern-bound birds, their pale and second-hand reports, had yet power to awaken this wild new sensation and thrill him through and through with it; what would one moment of the real thing work in him – one passionate touch of the real southern sun, one waft of the authentic odour? With closed eyes he dared to dream a moment in full abandonment, and when he looked again the river seemed steely and chill, the green fields grey and lightless. Then his loyal heart seemed to cry out on his weaker self for its treachery.

"Why do you ever come back, then, at all?" he demanded of the swallows jealously. "What do you find to attract you in this poor drab little country?"

"And do you think," said the first swallow, "that the other call is not for us too, in its due season? The call of lush meadow-grass, wet orchards, warm, insect-haunted ponds, of browsing cattle, of haymaking, and all the farm-buildings clustered round the House of the perfect Eaves?"

"Do you suppose," asked the second one, "that you are the only living thing that craves with a hungry longing to hear the cuckoo's note again?"

"In due time," said the third, "we shall be home-sick once more for quiet water-lilies swaying on the surface of an English stream. But to-day all that seems pale and thin and very far away. Just now our blood dances to other music."

They fell a-twittering among themselves once more, and this time their intoxicating babble was of violet seas, tawny sands, and lizard-haunted walls.

Restlessly the Rat wandered off once more, climbed the slope that rose gently from the north bank of the river, and lay looking out towards the great ring of Downs that barred his vision further southwards – his simple horizon hitherto, his Mountains of the Moon, his limit behind which lay nothing he had cared to see or to know. To-day, to him gazing south with a new-born need stirring in his heart, the clear sky over their long low outline seemed to pulsate with promise; to-day, the unseen was everything, the unknown the only real fact of life. On this side of the hills was now the real blank, on the other lay the crowded and coloured panorama that his inner eye was seeing so clearly. What seas lay beyond, green, leaping, and crested! What sun-bathed coasts, along which the white villas glittered against the olive woods! What quiet harbours, thronged with gallant shipping bound for purple islands of wine and spice, islands set low in languorous waters!

He rose and descended river-wards once more; then changed his mind and sought the side of the dusty lane. There, lying half-buried in the thick, cool under-hedge tangle that bordered it, he could muse on the metalled road and all the wondrous world that it led to; on all the wayfarers, too, that might have trodden it, and the fortunes and adventures they had gone to seek or found unseeking – out there, beyond – beyond!

Footsteps fell on his ear, and the figure of one that walked somewhat wearily came into view; and he saw that it was a Rat, and a very dusty one. The wayfarer, as he reached him, saluted with a gesture of courtesy that had something foreign about it – hesitated a moment – then with a pleasant smile turned from the track and sat down by his side in the cool herbage. He seemed tired, and the Rat let him rest unquestioned, understanding something of what was in his thoughts; knowing, too, the value all animals attach at times to mere silent companionship, when the weary muscles slacken and the mind marks time.

The wayfarer was lean and keen-featured, and somewhat bowed at the shoulders; his paws were thin and long, his eyes much wrinkled at the corners, and he wore small gold earrings in his neatly-set, well-shaped ears. His knitted jersey was of a faded blue, his breeches, patched and stained, were based on a blue foundation, and his small belongings that  he carried were tied up in a blue cotton handkerchief.

When he had rested awhile the stranger sighed, snuffed the air, and looked about him.

"That was clover, that warm whiff on the breeze," he remarked; "and those are cows we hear cropping the grass behind us and blowing softly between mouthfuls. There is a sound of distant reapers, and yonder rises a blue line of cottage smoke against the woodland. The river runs somewhere close by, for I hear the call of a moorhen, and I see by your build that you're a freshwater mariner. Everything seems asleep, and yet going on all the time. It is a goodly life that you lead, friend; no doubt the best in the world, if only you are strong enough to lead it!"

"Yes, it's *the* life, the only life, to live," responded the Water Rat dreamily, and without his usual whole-hearted conviction.

"I did not say exactly that," replied the stranger cautiously; "but no doubt it's the best. I've tried it, and I know. And because I've just tried it – six months of it – and know it's the best, here am I, footsore and hungry, tramping away from it, tramping southward, following the old call, back to the old life, *the* life which is mine and which will not let me go."

"Is this, then, yet another of them?" mused the Rat. "And where have you just come from?" he asked. He hardly dared to ask where he was bound for; he seemed to know the answer only too well.

"Nice little farm," replied the wayfarer, briefly. "Upalong in that direction" – he nodded northwards. "Never mind about it. I had everything I could want – everything I had any right to expect of life, and more; and here I am! Glad to be here all the same, though, glad to be here! So many miles further on the road, so many hours nearer to my heart's desire!"

His shining eyes held fast to the horizon, and he seemed to be listening for some sound that was wanting from that inland acreage, vocal as it was with the cheerful music of pasturage and farmyard.

"You are not one of *us*," said the Water Rat, "nor yet a farmer; nor even, I should judge, of this country."

"Right," replied the stranger. "I'm a seafaring rat, I am, and the port I originally hail from is Constantinople, though I'm a sort of a foreigner there too, in a manner of speaking. You will have heard of Constantinople, friend? A fair city, and an ancient and glorious one. And you may have heard, too, of Sigurd, King of Norway, and how he sailed thither with sixty ships, and how he and his men rode up through streets all canopied in their honour with purple and gold; and how the Emperor and Empress came down and banqueted with him on board his ship. When Sigurd returned home, many of his Northmen remained behind and entered the Emperor's bodyguard, and my ancestor, a Norwegian born, stayed behind too, with the ships that Sigurd gave the Emperor. Seafarers we have ever been, and no wonder; as for me, the city of my birth is no more my home than any pleasant port between there and the London River. I know them all, and they know me. Set me down on any of their quays or foreshores, and I am home again."

"I suppose you go great voyages," said the Water Rat with growing interest. "Months and months out of sight of land, and provisions running short, and allowanced as to water, and your mind communing with the mighty ocean, and all that sort of thing?"

"By no means," said the Sea Rat frankly. "Such a life as you describe would not suit me at all. I'm in the coasting trade, and rarely out of sight of land. It's the jolly times on shore that appeal to me, as much as any seafaring. O, those southern seaports! The smell of them, the riding-lights at night, the glamour!"

"Well, perhaps you have chosen the better way," said the Water Rat, but rather doubtfully. "Tell me something of your coasting, then, if you have a mind to, and what sort of harvest an animal of spirit might hope to bring home from it to warm his latter days with gallant memories by the fireside; for my life, I confess to you, feels to me to-day somewhat narrow and circumscribed."

"My last voyage," began the Sea Rat, "that landed me eventually in this country, bound with high hopes for my inland farm, will serve as a good example of any of them, and, indeed, as an epitome of my highly-coloured life. Family troubles, as usual, began it. The domestic storm-cone was hoisted, and I shipped myself on board a small trading vessel bound from Constantinople, by classic seas whose every wave throbs with a deathless memory, to the Grecian Islands and the Levant. Those were golden days and balmy nights! In and out of harbour all the time – old friends everywhere – sleeping in some cool temple or ruined cistern during the heat of the day – feasting and song after sundown, under great stars set in a velvet sky! Thence we turned and coasted up the Adriatic, its shores swimming in an atmosphere of amber, rose, and aquamarine;

we lay in wide land-locked harbours, we roamed through ancient and noble cities, until at last one morning, as the sun rose royally behind us, we rode into Venice down a path of gold. O, Venice is a fine city, wherein a rat can wander at his ease and take his pleasure! Or, when weary of wandering, can sit at the edge of the Grand Canal at night, feasting with his friends, when the air is full of music and the sky full of stars, and the lights flash and shimmer on the polished steel prows of the swaying gondolas, packed so that you could walk across the canal on them from side to side! And then the food – do you like shellfish? Well, well, we won't linger over that now."

He was silent for a time; and the Water Rat, silent too and enthralled, floated on dream-canals and heard a phantom song pealing high between vaporous grey wave-lapped walls.

"Southwards we sailed again at last," continued the Sea Rat, "coasting down the Italian shore, till finally we made Palermo, and there I quitted for a long, happy spell on shore. I never stick too long to one ship; one gets narrow-minded and prejudiced. Besides, Sicily is one of my happy hunting-grounds. I know everybody there, and their ways just suit me. I spent many jolly weeks in the island, staying with friends up country. When I grew restless again I took advantage of a ship that was trading to Sardinia and Corsica; and very glad I was to feel the fresh breeze and the sea-spray in my face once more."

"But isn't it very hot and stuffy, down in the – hold, I think you call it?" asked the Water Rat.

The seafarer looked at him with the suspicion of a wink. "I'm an old hand," he remarked with much simplicity. "The captain's cabin's good enough for me."

"It's a hard life, by all accounts," murmured the Rat, sunk in deep thought.

"For the crew it is," replied the seafarer gravely, again with the ghost of a wink.

"From Corsica," he went on, "I made use of a ship that was taking wine to the mainland. We made Alassio in the evening, lay to, hauled up our wine-casks, and hove them overboard, tied one to the other by a long line. Then the crew took to the boats and rowed shorewards, singing as they went, and drawing after them the long bobbing procession of casks, like a mile of porpoises. On the sands they had horses waiting, which dragged the casks up the steep street of the little town with a fine rush and clatter and scramble. When the last cask was in, we went and refreshed and rested, and sat late into the night, drinking with our friends, and next morning I was off to the great olive-woods for a spell and a rest. For now I had done with islands for the time, and ports and shipping were plentiful; so I led a lazy life among the peasants, lying and watching them work, or stretched high on the hillside with the blue Mediterranean far below me. And so at length, by easy stages, and partly on foot, partly by sea, to Marseilles, and the meeting of old shipmates, and the visiting of great ocean-bound vessels, and feasting once more. Talk of shellfish! Why, sometimes I dream of the shellfish of Marseilles, and wake up crying!"

"That reminds me," said the polite Water Rat; "you happened to mention that you were hungry, and I ought to have spoken earlier. Of course, you will

stop and take your midday meal with me? My hole is close by; it is some time past noon, and you are very welcome to whatever there is."

"Now I call that kind and brotherly of you," said the Sea Rat. "I was indeed hungry when I sat down, and ever since I inadvertently happened to mention shellfish, my pangs have been extreme. But couldn't you fetch it along out here? I am none too fond of going under hatches, unless I'm obliged to; and then, while we eat, I could tell you more concerning my voyages and the pleasant life I lead – at least, it is very pleasant to me, and by your attention I judge it commends itself to you; whereas if we go indoors it is a hundred to one that I shall presently fall asleep."

"That is indeed an excellent suggestion," said the Water Rat, and hurried off home. There he got out the luncheon-basket and packed a simple meal, in which, remembering the stranger's origin and preferences, he took care to include a yard of long French bread, a sausage out of which the garlic sang, some cheese which lay down and cried, and a long-necked straw-covered flask containing bottled sunshine shed and garnered on far Southern slopes. Thus laden, he returned with all speed, and blushed for pleasure at the old seaman's commendations of his taste and judgment, as together they unpacked the basket and laid out the contents on the grass by the roadside.

The Sea Rat, as soon as his hunger was somewhat assuaged, continued the history of his latest voyage, conducting his simple hearer from port to port of Spain, landing him at Lisbon, Oporto, and Bordeaux, introducing him to the pleasant harbours of Cornwall and Devon, and so up the Channel to that final quayside, where, landing after winds long contrary, storm-driven and weather-beaten, he had caught the first magical hints and heraldings of another spring, and, fired by these, had sped on a long tramp inland, hungry for the experiment of life on some quiet farmstead, very far from the weary beating of any sea.

Spellbound and quivering with excitement, the Water Rat followed the Adventurer league by league, over stormy bays, through crowded roadsteads, across harbour bars on a racing tide, up winding rivers that hid their busy little towns round a sudden turn; and left him with a regretful sigh planted at his dull inland farm, about which he desired to hear nothing.

By this time the meal was over, and the Seafarer, refreshed and strengthened, his voice more vibrant, his eye lit with a brightness that seemed caught from some far-away sea-beacon, filled his glass with the red and glowing vintage of the South, and, leaning towards the Water Rat, compelled his gaze and held him, body and soul, while he talked. Those eyes were of the changing foam-streaked grey-green of leaping Northern seas; in the glass shone a hot ruby that seemed the very heart of the South, beating for him who had courage to respond to its pulsation. The twin lights, the shifting grey and the steadfast red, mastered the Water Rat and held him bound, fascinated, powerless. The quiet world outside their rays receded far away and ceased to be. And the talk, the wonderful talk flowed on – or was it speech entirely, or did it pass at times into song – chanty of the sailors weighing the dripping anchor, sonorous hum of the shrouds in a tearing North-Easter, ballad of the fisherman hauling his nets at sundown against an apricot sky, chords of guitar and mandoline from gondola or caique? Did it change into the cry of the wind, plaintive at first, angrily shrill as it freshened, rising to a tearing whistle, sinking to a musical trickle of air from the leech of the bellying sail? All these sounds the spell-bound listener seemed to hear, and with them the hungry complaint of the gulls and the sea-mews, the soft thunder of the breaking wave, the cry of the protesting shingle. Back into speech again it passed, and with beating heart he was following the adventures of a dozen seaports, the fights, the escapes, the rallies, the comradeships, the gallant undertakings; or he searched islands for treasure, fished in still lagoons and dozed day-long on warm white sand. Of deep-sea fishings he heard tell, and mighty silver gatherings of the mile-long net; of sudden perils, noise of breakers on a moonless night, or the tall bows of the great liner taking shape overhead through the fog; of the merry home-coming, the headland rounded, the harbour lights opened out; the groups seen dimly on the quay, the cheery hail, the splash of the hawser; the trudge up the steep little street towards the comforting glow of red-curtained windows.

Lastly, in his waking dream it seemed to him that the Adventurer had risen to his feet, but was still speaking, still holding him fast with his sea-grey eyes.

"And now," he was softly saying, "I take to the road again, holding on south-westwards for many a long and dusty day; till at last, I reach the little grey sea town I know so well, that clings along one steep side of the harbour. There through dark doorways you look down flights of stone steps, overhung by great pink tufts of valerian and ending in a patch of sparkling blue water. The little boats that lie tethered to the rings and stanchions of the old sea-wall are gaily painted as those I clambered in and out of in my own childhood; the salmon leap on the flood tide, schools of mackerel flash and play past quaysides and foreshores, and by the windows the great vessels glide, night and day, up to their moorings or forth to the open sea. There, sooner or later, the ships of all seafaring nations arrive; and there, at its destined hour, the ship of my choice will let go its anchor. I shall take my time, I shall tarry and bide, till at last the right one lies waiting for me, warped out into midstream, loaded low, her bowsprit pointing down harbour. I shall slip on board, by boat or along hawser; and then one morning I shall wake to the song and tramp of the sailors, the clink of the capstan, and the rattle of the anchor-chain coming merrily in. We shall break out the jib and the foresail, the white houses on the harbour side will glide slowly past us as she gathers steering-way, and the voyage will have begun! As she forges towards the headland she will clothe herself with canvas; and then, once outside, the sounding slap of great green seas as she heels to the wind, pointing South!

"And you, you will come too, young brother; for the days pass, and never return, and the South still waits for you. Take the Adventure, heed the call, now ere the irrevocable moment passes! 'Tis but a banging of the door behind you, a blithesome step forward, and you are out of the old life and into the new! Then some day, some day long hence, jog home here if you will, when the cup has been drained and the play has been played, and sit down by your quiet river with a store of goodly memories for company. You can easily overtake me on the road, for you are young, and I am ageing and go softly. I will linger, and look back; and at last I will surely see you coming, eager and light-hearted, with all the South in your face!"

The voice died away and ceased, as an insect's tiny trumpet dwindles swiftly into silence; and the Water Rat, paralysed and staring, saw at last but a distant speck on the white surface of the road.

Mechanically he rose and proceeded to repack the luncheon-basket, carefully and without haste. Mechanically he returned home, gathered together a few small necessaries and special treasures he was fond of, and put them in a satchel; acting with slow deliberation, moving about the room like a sleep-walker; listening ever with parted lips. He swung the satchel over his shoulder, carefully selected a stout stick for his wayfaring, and with no haste, but with no hesitation at all, he stepped across the threshold just as the Mole appeared at the door.

"Why, where are you off to, Ratty?" asked the Mole in great surprise, grasping him by the arm.

"Going South, with the rest of them," murmured the Rat in a dreamy monotone, never looking at him. "Seawards first and then on shipboard, and so to the shores that are calling me!"

He pressed resolutely forward, still without haste, but with dogged fixity of purpose; but the Mole, now thoroughly alarmed, placed himself in front of him, and looking into his eyes saw that they were glazed and set and turned a streaked and shifting grey – not his friend's eyes, but the eyes of some other animal! Grappling with him strongly he dragged him inside, threw him down, and held him.

The Rat struggled desperately for a few moments, and then his strength seemed suddenly to leave him, and he lay still and exhausted, with closed eyes, trembling. Presently the Mole assisted him to rise and placed him in a chair, where he sat collapsed and shrunken into himself, his body shaken by a violent shivering, passing in time into an hysterical fit of dry sobbing. Mole made the door fast, threw the satchel into a drawer and locked it, and sat down quietly on the table by his friend, waiting for the strange seizure to pass. Gradually the Rat sank into a troubled doze, broken by starts and confused murmurings of things strange and wild and foreign to the unenlightened Mole; and from that he passed into a deep slumber.

Very anxious in mind, the Mole left him for a time and busied himself with household matters; and it was getting dark when he returned to the parlour and found the Rat where he had left him, wide awake indeed, but listless, silent, and dejected. He took one hasty glance at his eyes; found them, to his great gratification, clear and dark and brown again as before; and then sat down and tried to cheer him up and help him to relate what had happened to him.

Poor Ratty did his best, by degrees, to explain things; but how could he put into cold words what had mostly been suggestion? How recall, for another's benefit, the haunting sea voices that had sung to him, how reproduce at second-hand the magic of the Seafarer's hundred reminiscences? Even to himself, now the spell was broken and the glamour gone, he found it difficult to account for what had seemed, some hours ago, the inevitable and only thing. It is not surprising, then, that he failed to convey to the Mole any clear idea of what he had been through that day.

To the Mole this much was plain: the fit, or attack, had passed away, and had left him sane again, though shaken and cast down by the reaction. But he seemed to have lost all interest for the time in the things that went to make up his daily life, as well as in all pleasant forecastings of the altered days and doings that the changing season was surely bringing.

Casually, then, and with seeming indifference, the Mole turned his talk to the harvest that was being gathered in, the towering wagons and their straining teams, the growing ricks, and the large moon rising over bare acres dotted with sheaves. He talked of the reddening apples around, of the browning nuts, of jams and preserves and the distilling of cordials; till by easy stages such as these he reached midwinter, its hearty joys and its snug home life, and then he became simply lyrical.

By degrees the Rat began to sit up and to join in. His dull eyes brightened, and he lost some of his listless air.

Presently the tactful Mole slipped away and returned with a pencil and a few half-sheets of paper, which he placed on the table at his friend's elbow.

"It's quite a long time since you did any poetry," he remarked. "You might have a try at it this evening, instead of – well, brooding over things so much. I've an idea that you'll feel a lot better when you've got something jotted down – if it's only just the rhymes."

The Rat pushed the paper away from him wearily, but the discreet Mole took occasion to leave the room, and when he peeped in again some time later, the Rat was absorbed and deaf to the world; alternately scribbling and sucking the top of his pencil. It is true that he sucked a good deal more than he scribbled; but it was a joy to the Mole to know that the cure had at least begun.

Chapter 10

The Further Adventures of Toad

The front door of the hollow tree faced eastwards, so Toad was called at an early hour; partly by the bright sunlight streaming in on him, partly by the exceeding coldness of his toes, which made him dream that he was at home in bed in his own handsome room with the Tudor window, on a cold winter's night, and his bedclothes had got up, grumbling and protesting they couldn't stand the cold any longer, and had run downstairs to the kitchen fire to warm themselves; and he had followed, on bare feet, along miles and miles of icy stone-paved passages, arguing and beseeching them to be reasonable. He would probably have been aroused much earlier, had he not slept for some weeks on straw over stone flags, and almost forgotten the friendly feeling of thick blankets pulled well up round the chin.

Sitting up, he rubbed his eyes first and his complaining toes next, wondered for a moment where he was, looking round for a familiar stone wall and little barred window; then, with a leap of the heart, remembered everything – his escape, his flight, his pursuit; remembered, first and best thing of all, that he was free!

Free! The word and the thought alone were worth fifty blankets. He was warm from end to end as he thought of the jolly world outside, waiting eagerly for him to make his triumphal entrance, ready to serve him and play up to him, anxious to help him and to keep him company, as it always had been in days of old before misfortune fell upon him. He shook himself and combed the dry leaves out of his hair with his fingers; and, his toilet complete, marched forth into the comfortable morning sun, cold but confident, hungry but hopeful, all nervous terrors of yesterday dispelled by rest and sleep and frank and heartening sunshine.

He had the world all to himself, that early summer morning. The dewy woodland, as he threaded it, was solitary and still: the green fields that succeeded the trees were his own to do as he liked with; the road itself, when he reached it, in that loneliness that was everywhere, seemed, like a stray dog, to be looking anxiously for company. Toad, however, was looking for something that could talk, and tell him clearly which way he ought to go. It is all very well, when you have a light heart, and a clear conscience, and money in your pocket, and nobody scouring the country for you to drag you off to prison again, to follow where the road beckons and points, not caring whither. The practical Toad cared very much indeed, and he could have kicked the road for its helpless silence when every minute was of importance to him.

The reserved rustic road was presently joined by a shy little brother in the shape of a canal, which took its hand and ambled along by its side in perfect confidence, but with the same tongue-tied, uncommunicative attitude towards strangers. "Bother them!" said Toad to himself. "But, anyhow, one thing's clear. They must both be coming *from* somewhere, and going *to* somewhere. You can't get over that, Toad, my boy!" So he marched on patiently by the water's edge.

Round a bend in the canal came plodding a solitary horse, stooping forward as if in anxious thought. From rope traces attached to his collar stretched a long line, taut, but dipping with his stride, the further part of it dripping pearly drops. Toad let the horse pass, and stood waiting for what the fates were sending him.

With a pleasant swirl of quiet water at its blunt bow the barge slid up alongside of him, its gaily painted gunwale level with the towing-path, its sole occupant a big stout woman wearing a linen sun-bonnet, one brawny arm laid along the tiller.

"A nice morning, ma'am!" she remarked to Toad, as she drew up level with him.

"I dare say it is, ma'am!" responded Toad politely, as he walked along the tow-path abreast of her. "I dare it *is* a nice morning to them that's not in sore trouble, like what I am. Here's my married daughter, she sends off to me post-haste to come to her at once; so off I comes, not knowing what may be happening or going to happen, but fearing the worst, as you will understand, ma'am, if you're a mother, too. And I've left my business to look after itself – I'm in the washing and laundering line, you must know, ma'am – and I've left my young children to look after themselves, and a more mischievous and troublesome set of young imps doesn't exist, ma'am; and I've lost all my money, and lost my way, and as for what may be happening to my married daughter, why, I don't like to think of it, ma'am!"

"Where might your married daughter be living, ma'am?" asked the barge-woman.

"She lives near to the river, ma'am," replied Toad. "Close to a fine house called Toad Hall, that's somewheres hereabouts in these parts. Perhaps you may have heard of it."

"Toad Hall? Why, I'm going that way myself," replied the barge-woman. "This canal joins the river some miles further on, a little above Toad Hall; and then it's an easy walk. You come along in the barge with me, and I'll give you a lift."

She steered the barge close to the bank, and Toad, with many humble and grateful acknowledgments, stepped lightly on board and sat down with great satisfaction. "Toad's luck again!" thought he. "I always come out on top!"

"So you're in the washing business, ma'am?" said the barge-woman politely, as they glided along. "And a very good business you've got too, I dare say, if I'm not making too free in saying so."

"Finest business in the whole country," said Toad airily. "All the gentry come to me – wouldn't go to anyone else if they were paid, they know me so well. You see, I understand my work thoroughly, and attend to it all myself. Washing, ironing, clear-starching, making up gents' fine shirts for evening wear – everything's done under my own eye!"

"But surely you don't do all that work yourself, ma'am?" asked the barge-woman respectfully.

"O, I have girls," said Toad lightly: "twenty girls or thereabouts, always at work. But you know what *girls* are, ma'am! Nasty little hussies, that's what *I* call 'em!"

"So do I, too," said the barge-woman with great heartiness. "But I dare say you set yours to rights, the idle trollops! And are you *very* fond of washing?"

"I love it," said Toad. "I simply dote on it. Never so happy as when I've got both arms in the wash-tub. But, then, it comes so easy to me! No trouble at all! A real pleasure, I assure you, ma'am!"

"What a bit of luck, meeting you!" observed the barge-woman, thoughtfully. "A regular piece of good fortune for both of us!"

"Why, what do you mean?" asked Toad, nervously.

"Well, look at me, now," replied the barge-woman. "*I* like washing, too, just the same as you do; and for that matter, whether I like it or not I have got to do all my own, naturally, moving about as I do. Now my husband, he's such a fellow for shirking his work and leaving the barge to me, that never a moment do I get for seeing to my own affairs. By rights he ought to be here now, either steering or attending to the horse, though luckily the horse has sense enough to attend to himself. Instead of which, he's gone off with the dog, to see if they can't pick up a rabbit for dinner somewhere. Says he'll catch me up at the next lock. Well, that's as may be – I don't trust him, once he gets off with that dog, who's worse than he is. But meantime, how am I to get on with my washing?"

"O, never mind about the washing," said Toad, not liking the subject. "Try and fix your mind on that rabbit. A nice fat young rabbit, I'll be bound. Got any onions?"

"I can't fix my mind on anything but my washing," said the barge-woman, "and I wonder you can be talking of rabbits, with such a joyful prospect before you. There's a heap of things of mine that you'll find in a corner of the cabin. If you'll just take one or two of the most necessary sort – I won't venture to describe them to a lady like you, but you'll recognize 'em at a glance – and put them through the wash-tub as we go along, why, it'll be a pleasure to you, as you rightly say, and a real help to me. You'll find a tub handy, and soap, and a kettle on the stove, and a bucket to haul up water from the canal with. Then I shall know you're enjoying yourself, instead of sitting here idle, looking at the scenery and yawning your head off."

"Here, you let me steer!" said Toad, now thoroughly frightened, "and then you can get on with your washing your own way. I might spoil your things, or not do 'em as you like. I'm more used to gentlemen's things myself. It's my special line."

"Let you steer?" replied the barge-woman, laughing. "It takes some practice to steer a barge properly. Besides, it's dull work, and I want you to be happy. No, you shall do the washing you are so fond of, and I'll stick to the steering that I understand. Don't try and deprive me of the pleasure of giving you a treat!"

Toad was fairly cornered. He looked for escape this way and that, saw that he was too far from the bank for a flying leap, and sullenly resigned himself to his fate. "If it comes to that," he thought in desperation, "I suppose any fool can *wash*!"

He fetched tub, soap, and other necessaries from the cabin, selected a few garments at random, tried to recollect what he had seen in casual glances through laundry windows, and set to.

A long half-hour passed, and every minute of it saw Toad getting crosser and crosser. Nothing that he could do to the things seemed to please them or do them good. He tried coaxing, he tried slapping, he tried punching; they smiled back at him out of the tub unconverted, happy in their original sin. Once or twice he looked nervously over his shoulder at the barge-woman, but she appeared to be gazing out in front of her, absorbed in her steering. His back ached badly, and he noticed with dismay that his paws were beginning to get all crinkly. Now Toad was very proud of his paws. He muttered under his breath words that should never pass the lips of either washerwomen or Toads; and lost the soap, for the fiftieth time.

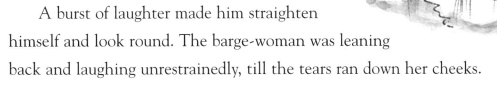

A burst of laughter made him straighten himself and look round. The barge-woman was leaning back and laughing unrestrainedly, till the tears ran down her cheeks.

"I've been watching you all the time," she gasped. "I thought you must be a humbug all along, from the conceited way you talked. Pretty washerwoman you are! Never washed so much as a dish-clout in your life, I'll lay!"

Toad's temper which had been simmering viciously for some time, now fairly boiled over, and he lost all control of himself.

"You common, low, *fat* barge-woman!" he shouted; "don't you dare to talk to your betters like that! Washerwoman indeed! I would have you to know that I am a Toad, a very well-known, respected, distinguished Toad! I may be under a bit of a cloud at present, but I will *not* be laughed at by a barge-woman!"

The woman moved nearer to him and peered under his bonnet keenly and closely. "Why, so you are!" she cried. "Well, I never! A horrid, nasty, crawly

Toad! And in my nice clean barge, too! Now that is a thing that I will *not* have."

She relinquished the tiller for a moment. One big mottled arm shot out and caught Toad by a fore-leg, while the other gripped him fast by a hind-leg. Then the world turned suddenly upside down, the barge seemed to flit lightly across the sky, the wind whistled in his ears, and Toad found himself flying through the air, revolving rapidly as he went.

The water, when he eventually reached it with a loud splash, proved quite cold enough for his taste, though its chill was not sufficient to quell his proud spirit, or slake the heat of his furious temper. He rose to the surface spluttering, and when he had wiped the duck-weed out of his eyes the first thing he saw was the fat barge-woman looking back at him over the stern of the retreating barge and laughing; and he vowed, as he coughed and choked, to be even with her.

He struck out for the shore, but the cotton gown greatly impeded his efforts, and when at length he touched land he found it hard to climb up the steep bank unassisted. He had to take a minute or two's rest to recover his breath; then, gathering his wet skirts well over his arms, he started to run after the barge as fast as his legs would carry him. Wild with indignation, thirsting for revenge.

The barge-woman was still laughing when he drew up level with her. "Put yourself through your mangle, washerwoman," she called out, "and iron your face and crimp it, and you'll pass for quite a decent-looking Toad!"

Toad never paused to reply. Solid revenge was what he wanted, not cheap, windy, verbal triumphs, though he had a thing or two in his mind that he would have liked to say. He saw what he wanted ahead of him. Running swiftly on he overtook the horse, unfastened the tow-rope and cast off, jumped lightly on the horse's back, and urged it to a gallop by kicking it vigorously in the sides. He steered for the open country, abandoning the tow-path, and swinging his steed down a rutty lane. Once he looked back, and saw that the barge had run aground on the other side of the canal, and the barge-woman was gesticulating wildly and shouting "Stop, stop, stop!"

"I've heard that song before," said Toad, laughing, as he continued to spur his steed onward in its wild career.

The barge-horse was not capable of any very sustained effort, and its gallop soon subsided into a trot, and its trot into an easy walk; but Toad was quite contented with this, knowing that he, at any rate, was moving, and the barge was not. He had quite recovered his temper, now that he had done something he thought really clever; and he was satisfied to jog along quietly in the sun, taking advantage of any by-ways and bridle-paths, and trying to forget how very long it was since he had had a square meal, till the canal had been left very far behind him.

He had travelled some miles, his horse and he, and he was feeling drowsy in the hot sunshine, when the horse stopped, lowered his head, and began to nibble the grass; and Toad, waking up, just saved himself from falling off by an effort. He looked about him and found he was on a wide common, dotted with patches of gorse and bramble as far as he could see. Near him stood a dingy gipsy caravan, and beside it a man was sitting on a bucket turned upside down, very busy smoking and staring into the wide world. A fire of sticks was burning nearby, and over the fire hung an iron pot, and out of that pot came forth bubblings and gurglings, and a vague suggestive steaminess. Also smells – warm, rich, and varied smells – that twined and twisted and wreathed themselves at last into one complete, voluptuous, perfect smell that seemed like the very soul of Nature taking form and appearing to her children, a true Goddess, a mother of solace and comfort. Toad now knew well that he had not been really hungry before. What he had felt earlier in the day had been a mere trifling qualm. This was the real thing at last, and no mistake; and it would have to be dealt with speedily, too, or there would be trouble for somebody or something. He looked the gipsy over carefully, wondering vaguely whether it would be easier to fight him or cajole him. So there he sat, and sniffed and sniffed, and looked at the gipsy; and the gipsy sat and smoked, and looked at him.

Presently the gipsy took his pipe out of his mouth and remarked in a careless way, "Want to sell that there horse of yours?"

Toad was completely taken back. He did not know that gipsies were very fond of horse-dealing, and never missed an opportunity, and he had not reflected that caravans were always on the move and took a deal of drawing. It had not occurred to him to turn the horse into cash, but the gipsy's suggestion seemed to smooth the way towards the two things he wanted so badly – ready money, and a solid breakfast.

"What?" he said, "me sell this beautiful young horse of mine? O, no; it's out of the question. Who's going to take the washing home to my customers every week? Besides, I'm too fond of him, and he simply dotes on me."

"Try and love a donkey," suggested the gipsy. "Some people do."

"You don't seem to see," continued Toad, "that this fine horse of mine is a cut above you altogether. He's a blood horse, he is, partly; not the part you see, of course – another part. And he's been a Prize Hackney, too, in his time – that was the time before you knew him, but you can still tell it on him at a glance, if you understand anything about horses. No, it's not to be thought of for a moment. All the same, how much might you be disposed to offer me for this beautiful young horse of mine?"

The gipsy looked the horse over, and then he looked Toad over with equal care, and looked at the horse again. "Shillin' a leg," he said briefly, and turned away, continuing to smoke and try to stare the wide world out of countenance.

"A shilling a leg?" cried Toad. "If you please, I must take a little time to work that out, and see just what it comes to."

He climbed down off his horse, and left it to graze, and sat down by the gipsy, and did sums on his fingers, and at last he said, "A shilling a leg? Why, that comes to exactly four shillings, and no more. O, no; I could not think of accepting four shillings for this beautiful young horse of mine."

"Well," said the gipsy, "I'll tell you what I will do. I'll make it five shillings, and that's three-and-sixpence more than the animal's worth. And that's my last word."

Then Toad sat and pondered long and deeply. For he was hungry and quite penniless, and still some way – he knew not how far – from home, and enemies might still be looking for him. To one in such a situation, five shillings may very well appear a large sum of money. On the other hand, it did not seem very much to get for a horse. But then, again, the horse hadn't cost him anything; so whatever he got was all clear profit. At last he said firmly, "Look here, gipsy! I tell you what we will do; and this is *my* last word. You shall hand me over six shillings and sixpence, cash down; and further, in addition thereto, you shall give me as much breakfast as I can possibly eat, at one sitting of course, out of that iron pot of yours that keeps sending forth such delicious and exciting smells. In return, I will make over to you my spirited young horse, with all the beautiful harness and trappings that are on him, freely thrown in. If that's not good enough for you, say so, and I'll be getting on. I know a man near here who's wanted this horse of mine for years."

The gipsy grumbled frightfully, and declared if he did a few more deals of that sort he'd be ruined. But in the end he lugged a dirty canvas bag out of the depths of his trouser pocket, and counted out six shillings and sixpence into Toad's paw. Then he disappeared into the caravan for an instant, and returned with a large iron plate and a knife, fork and spoon. He tilted up the pot, and a glorious stream of hot rich stew gurgled into the plate. It was, indeed, the most beautiful stew in the world, being made of partridges, and pheasants, and chickens, and hares, and rabbits, and peahens, and guinea-fowls, and one or two other things. Toad

took the plate on his lap, almost crying, and stuffed, and stuffed, and stuffed, and kept asking for more, and the gipsy never grudged it him. He thought that he had never eaten so good a breakfast in all his life.

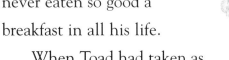

When Toad had taken as much stew on board as he thought he could possibly hold, he got up and said goodbye to the gipsy, and took an affectionate farewell of the horse; and the gipsy, who knew the riverside well, gave him directions which way to go, and he set forth on his travels again in the best possible spirits. He was, indeed, a very different Toad from the animal of an hour ago. The sun was shining brightly, his wet clothes were quite dry again, he had money in his pocket once more, he was nearing home and friends and safety, and, most and best of all, he had had a substantial meal, hot and nourishing, and felt big, and strong, and careless, and self-confident.

As he tramped along gaily, he thought of his adventures and escapes, and how when things seemed at their worst he had always managed to find a way out; and his pride and conceit began to swell within him. "Ho, ho!" he said to himself as he marched along with his chin in the air, "what a clever Toad I am! There is surely no animal equal to me for cleverness in the whole world! My enemies shut me up in prison, encircled by sentries, watched night and day by warders; I walk out through them all, by sheer ability coupled with courage. They pursue me with engines, and policemen, and revolvers; I snap my fingers at them, and vanish, laughing, into space. I am, unfortunately, thrown into a canal by a woman fat of body and very evil-minded. What of it? I swim ashore, I seize her horse, I ride off in triumph, and I sell the horse for a whole pocketful of money and an excellent breakfast! Ho, ho! I am The Toad, the handsome, the popular, the successful Toad!" He got so puffed up with conceit that he made up a song as he walked in praise of himself, and sang it at the top of his voice, though there was no one to hear it but him. It was perhaps the most conceited song that any animal ever composed.

"The world has held great Heroes,
　　As history-books have showed;
But never a name to go down to fame
　　Compared with that of Toad!

"The clever men at Oxford
    Know all that there is to be knowed.
But they none of them know one half as much
    As intelligent Mr Toad!

"The animals sat in the Ark and cried,
    Their tears in torrents flowed.
Who was it said, 'There's land ahead' ?
    Encouraging Mr Toad!

"The army all saluted
    As they marched along the road.
Was it the King? Or Kitchener?
    No. It was Mr Toad!

"The Queen and her Ladies-in-waiting
    Sat at the window and sewed.
She cried, 'Look! who's that *handsome* man?'
    They answered, 'Mr Toad'."

There was a great deal more of the same sort, but too dreadfully conceited to be written down. These are some of the milder verses.

He sang as he walked, and he walked as he sang, and got more inflated every minute. But his pride was shortly to have a severe fall.

After some miles of country lanes he reached the high road, and as he turned into it and glanced along its white length, he saw approaching him a speck that turned into a dot and then into a blob, and then into something very familiar; and a double note of warning, only too well-known, fell on his delighted ear.

"This is something like!" said the excited Toad. "This is real life again, this is once more the great world from which I have been missed so long! I will hail them, my brothers of the wheel, and pitch them a yarn, of the sort that has been so successful hitherto; and they will give me a lift, of course, and then I will talk to them some more; and, perhaps, with luck, it may even end in my driving up to Toad Hall in a motor-car! That will be one in the eye for Badger!"

He stepped confidently out into the road to hail the motor-car, which came along at an easy pace, slowing down as it neared the lane; when suddenly he became very pale, his heart turned to water, his knees shook and yielded under him, and he doubled up and collapsed with a sickening pain in his interior. And well he might, the unhappy animal; for the approaching car was the very one he had stolen out of the yard of the Red Lion Hotel on that fatal day when all his troubles began! And the people in it were the very same people he had sat and watched at luncheon in the coffee-room!

He sank down in a shabby, miserable heap in the road, murmuring to himself in his despair, "It's all up! It's all over now! Chains and policemen again! Prison again! Dry bread and water again! O, what a fool I have been! What did I want to go strutting about the country for, singing conceited songs, and hailing people in broad day on the high road, instead of hiding till nightfall and slipping home quietly by back ways! O hapless Toad! O ill-fated animal!"

The terrible motor-car drew slowly nearer and nearer, till at last he heard it stop just short of him. Two gentlemen got out and walked round the trembling heap of crumpled misery lying in the road, and one of them said, "O dear! this is very sad! Here is a poor old thing – a washerwoman, apparently – who has fainted in the road! Perhaps she is overcome by the heat, poor creature; or possibly she has not had any food to-day. Let us lift her into the car and take her to the nearest village, where doubtless she has friends."

They tenderly lifted Toad into the motor-car and propped him up with soft cushions, and proceeded on their way.

When Toad heard them talk in so kind and sympathetic a manner, and knew that he was not recognized, his courage began to revive, and he cautiously opened first one eye and then the other.

"Look!" said one of the gentlemen, "she is better already. The fresh air is doing her good. How do you feel now, ma'am?"

"Thank you kindly, sir," said Toad in a feeble voice, "I'm feeling a great deal better!"

"That's right," said the gentleman. "Now keep quite still, and, above all, don't try to talk."

"I won't," said Toad. "I was only thinking, if I might sit on the front seat there, beside the driver, where I could get the fresh air full in my face, I should soon be all right again."

"What a very sensible woman!" said the gentleman. "Of course you shall." So they carefully helped Toad into the front seat beside the driver, and on they went once more.

Toad was almost himself again by now. He sat up, looked about him, and tried to beat down the tremors, the yearnings, the old cravings that rose up and beset him and took possession of him entirely.

"It is fate!" he said to himself. "Why strive? why struggle?" and he turned to the driver at his side.

"Please, sir," he said, "I wish you would kindly let me try and drive the car for a little. I've been watching you carefully, and it looks so easy and so interesting, and I should like to be able to tell my friends that once I had driven a motor-car!"

The driver laughed at the proposal, so heartily that the gentleman inquired what the matter was. When he heard, he said, to Toad's delight, "Bravo, ma'am! I like your spirit. Let her have a try, and look after her. She won't do any harm." Toad eagerly scrambled into the seat vacated by the driver, took the steering-wheel in his hands, listened with affected humility to the instructions given him, and set the car in motion, but very slowly and carefully at first, for he was determined to be prudent. The gentlemen behind clapped their hands and applauded, and Toad heard them saying, "How well she does it! Fancy a washerwoman driving a car as well as that, the first time!"

Toad went a little faster; then faster still, and faster.

He heard the gentlemen call out warningly, "Be careful, washerwoman!" And this annoyed him, and he began to lose his head. The driver tried to interfere, but he pinned him down in his seat with one elbow, and put on full speed. The rush of air in his face, the hum of the engine, and the light jump of the car beneath him intoxicated his weak brain. "Washerwoman, indeed!" he shouted recklessly. "Ho! ho! I am the Toad, the motor-car snatcher, the prison-breaker, the Toad who always escapes! Sit still, and you shall know what driving really is, for you are in the hands of the famous, the skilful, the entirely fearless Toad!"

With a cry of horror the whole party rose and flung themselves on him. "Seize him!" they cried, "seize the Toad, the wicked animal who stole our motor-car! Bind him, chain him, drag him to the nearest police-station! Down with the desperate and dangerous Toad!"

Alas! they should have thought, they ought to have been more prudent, they should have remembered to stop the motor-car somehow before playing any pranks of that sort. With a half-turn of the wheel the Toad sent the car crashing through the low hedge that ran along the roadside. One mighty bound, a violent shock, and the wheels of the car were churning up the thick mud of a horse-pond.

Toad found himself flying through the air with the strong upward rush and delicate curve of a swallow. He liked the motion, and was just beginning to wonder whether it would go on until he developed wings and turned into a Toad-bird, when he landed on his back with a thump, in the soft rich grass of a meadow. Sitting up, he could just see the motor-car in the pond, nearly submerged; the gentlemen and the driver, encumbered by their long coats, were floundering helplessly in the water.

He picked himself up rapidly, and set off running across country as hard as he could, scrambling through hedges, jumping ditches, pounding across fields, till he was breathless and weary, and had to settle down into an easy walk. When he had recovered his breath somewhat, and was able to think calmly, he began to giggle, and from giggling he took to laughing, and he laughed till he had to sit down under a hedge. "Ho, ho!" he cried, in ecstasies of self-admiration, "Toad again! Toad, as usual, comes out on the top! Who was it got them to give him a lift? Who managed to get on the front seat for the sake of fresh air? Who persuaded them into letting him see if he could drive? Who landed them all in a horse-pond? Who escaped, flying gaily and unscathed through the air, leaving the narrow-minded, grudging, timid excursionists in the mud where they should rightly be? Why, Toad, of course; clever Toad, great Toad, *good* Toad!"

Then he burst into song again, and chanted with uplifted voice –

"The motor-car went Poop-poop-poop,
    As it raced along the road.
Who was it steered it into a pond?
    Ingenious Mr Toad!

"O, how clever I am! How clever, how clever, how very clev –"

A slight noise at a distance behind him made him turn his head and look. O horror! O misery! O despair!

About two fields off, a chauffeur in his leather gaiters and two large rural policemen were visible, running towards him as hard as they could go!

Poor Toad sprang to his feet and pelted away again, his heart in his mouth. "O, my!" he gasped, as he panted along, "what an *ass* I am! What a *conceited* and heedless ass! Swaggering again! Shouting and singing songs again! Sitting still and gassing again! O my! O my! O my!"

He glanced back, and saw to his dismay that they were gaining on him. On he ran desperately, but kept looking back, and saw that they still gained steadily. He did his best, but he was a fat animal, and his legs were short, and still they gained. He could hear them close behind him now. Ceasing to heed where he was going, he struggled on blindly and wildly, looking back over his shoulder at the now triumphant enemy, when suddenly the earth failed under his feet, he grasped at the air, and, splash! he found himself head over ears in deep water, rapid water, water that bore him along with a force he could not contend with; and he knew that in his blind panic he had run straight into the river!

He rose to the surface and tried to grasp the reeds and the rushes that grew along the water's edge close under the bank, but the stream was so strong that it tore them out of his hands. "O my!" gasped poor Toad, "if ever I steal a motor-car again! If ever I sing another conceited song" – then down he went, and came up breathless and spluttering. Presently he saw that he was approaching a big dark hole in the bank, just above his head, and as the stream bore him past he reached up with a paw and caught hold of the edge and held on. Then slowly and with difficulty he drew himself up out of the water, till at last he was able to rest his elbows on the edge of the hole. There he remained for some minutes, puffing and panting, for he was quite exhausted.

As he sighed and blew and stared before him into the dark hole, some bright small thing shone and twinkled in its depths, moving towards him. As it approached, a face grew up gradually around it, and it was a familiar face!

Brown and small, with whiskers.

Grave and round, with neat ears and silky hair. It was the Water Rat!

Chapter 11

"Like Summer Tempests Came his Tears"

The Rat put out a neat little brown paw, gripped Toad firmly by the scruff of the neck, and gave a great hoist and a pull; and the water-logged Toad came up slowly but surely over the edge of the hole, till at last he stood safe and sound in the hall, streaked with mud and weed to be sure, and with the water streaming off him, but happy and high-spirited as of old, now that he found himself once more in the house of a friend, and dodgings and evasions were over, and he could lay aside a disguise that was unworthy of his position and wanted such a lot of living up to.

"O, Ratty!" he cried. "I've been through such times since I saw you last, you can't think! Such trials, such sufferings, and all so nobly borne! Then such escapes, such disguises such subterfuges, and all so cleverly planned and carried out! Been in prison – got out of it, of course! Been thrown into a canal – swam ashore! Stole a horse – sold him for a large sum of money! Humbugged everybody – made 'em all do exactly what I wanted! O, I *am* a smart Toad, and no mistake! What do you think my last exploit was? Just hold on till I tell you –"

"Toad," said the Water Rat, gravely and firmly, "you go off upstairs at once, and take off that old cotton rag that looks as if it might formerly have belonged to some washerwoman, and clean yourself thoroughly, and put on some of my clothes, and try and come down looking like a gentleman if you *can*; for a more shabby, bedraggled, disreputable-looking object than you are I never set eyes on in my whole life! Now, stop swaggering and arguing, and be off! I'll have something to say to you later!"

Toad was at first inclined to stop and do some talking back at him. He had had enough of being ordered about when he was in prison, and here was the thing being begun all over again, apparently; and by a Rat, too! However, he caught sight of himself in the looking-glass over the hat-stand, with the rusty black bonnet perched rakishly over one eye, and he changed his mind and went very quickly and humbly upstairs to the Rat's dressing-room. There he had a thorough wash and brush-up, changed his clothes, and stood for a long time before the glass, contemplating himself with pride and pleasure, and thinking what utter idiots all the people must have been to have ever mistaken him for one moment for a washerwoman.

By the time he came down again luncheon was on the table, and very glad Toad was to see it, for he had been through some trying experiences and had taken much hard exercise since the excellent breakfast provided for him by the gipsy. While they ate Toad told the Rat all his adventures, dwelling chiefly on his own cleverness, and presence of mind in emergencies, and cunning in tight places; and rather making out that he had been having a gay and highly-coloured experience. But the more he talked and boasted, the more grave and silent the Rat became.

When at last Toad had talked himself to a standstill, there was silence for a while; and then the Rat said, "Now, Toady, I don't want to give you pain, after all you've been through already; but seriously, don't you see what an awful ass you've been making of yourself? On your own admission you have been handcuffed, imprisoned, starved, chased, terrified out of your life, insulted, jeered at, and ignominiously flung into the water – by a woman too! Where's the amusement in that? Where does the fun come in? And all because you must needs go and steal a motor-car. You know that you've never had anything but trouble from motor-cars from the moment you first set eyes on one. But if you *will* be mixed up with them – as you generally are, five minutes after you've started – why *steal* them? Be a cripple, if you think it's exciting; be a bankrupt, for a change, if you've set your mind on it: but why choose to be a convict? When are you going to be sensible, and think of your friends, and try and be a credit to them? Do you suppose it's any pleasure to me, for instance, to hear animals saying, as I go about, that I'm the chap that keeps company with gaol-birds?"

Now, it was a very comforting point in Toad's character that he was a thoroughly good-hearted animal and never minded being jawed by those who were his real friends. And even when most set upon a thing, he was always able to see the other side of the question. So although, while the Rat was talking so seriously, he kept saying to himself mutinously, "But it *was* fun, though! Awful fun!" and making strange suppressed noises inside him, k-i-ck-ck-ck, and poop-p-p, and other sounds resembling stifled snorts, or the opening of soda-water bottles, yet when the Rat had quite finished, he heaved a deep sigh and said, very nicely and humbly, "Quite right, Ratty! How *sound* you always are! Yes, I've been a conceited old ass, I can quite see that; but now I'm going to be a good Toad, and not do it any more. As for motor-cars, I've not been at all so keen about them since my last ducking in that river of yours. The fact is, while I was hanging on to the edge of your hole and getting my breath, I had a sudden idea – a really brilliant idea – connected with motor-boats – there, there! don't take on so, old chap, and stamp, and upset things; it was only an idea, and we won't talk any more about it now. We'll have our coffee, *and* a smoke, and a quiet chat, and then I'm going to stroll gently down to Toad Hall, and get into clothes of my own, and set things going again on the old lines. I've had enough of adventures. I shall lead a quiet, steady, respectable life, pottering about my property, and improving it, and doing a little landscape gardening at times. There will always be a bit of dinner for my friends when they come to see me; and I shall keep a pony-chaise to jog about the country in, just as I used to in the good old days, before I got restless, and wanted to *do* things."

"Stroll gently down to Toad Hall?" cried the Rat, greatly excited. "What are you talking about? Do you mean to say you haven't *heard?*"

"Heard what?" said Toad, turning rather pale. "Go on, Ratty! Quick! Don't spare me! What haven't I heard?"

"Do you mean to tell me," shouted the Rat, thumping with his little fist upon the table, "that you've heard nothing about the Stoats and Weasels?"

"What, the Wild Wooders?" cried Toad, trembling in every limb. "No, not a word! What have they been doing?"

"– And how they've been and taken Toad Hall?" continued the Rat.

Toad leant his elbows on the table, and his chin on his paws; and a large tear welled up in each of his eyes, overflowed and splashed on the table, plop! plop!

"Go on, Ratty," he murmured presently; "tell me all. The worst is over. I am an animal again. I can bear it."

"When you – got – into that – that – trouble of yours," said the Rat, slowly and impressively; "I mean, when you – disappeared from society for a time, over that misunderstanding about a – a machine, you know –"

Toad merely nodded.

"Well, it was a good deal talked about down here, naturally," continued the

Rat, "not only along the riverside, but even in the Wild Wood. Animals took sides, as always happens. The river-bankers stuck up for you, and said you had been infamously treated, and there was no justice to be had in the land nowadays. But the Wild Wood animals said hard things, and served you right, and it was time this sort of thing was stopped. And they got very cocky, and went about saying you were done for this time! You would never come back again, never, never!"

Toad nodded once more, keeping silence.

"That's the sort of little beasts they are," the Rat went on. "But Mole and Badger, they stuck out, through thick and thin, that you would come back again soon, somehow. They didn't know exactly how, but somehow! –"

Toad began to sit up in his chair again, and to smirk a little.

"They argued from history," continued the Rat. "They said that no criminal laws had ever been known to prevail against cheek and plausibility such as yours, combined with the power of a long purse. So they arranged to move their things into Toad Hall, and sleep there, and keep it aired, and have it all ready for you when you turned up. They didn't guess what was going to happen, of course; still, they had their suspicions of the Wild Wood animals. Now I come to the most painful and tragic part of my story. One dark night – it was a *very* dark night, and blowing hard, too, and raining simply cats and dogs – a band of weasels, armed to the teeth, crept silently up the carriage drive to the front entrance. Simultaneously, a body of desperate ferrets, advancing through the kitchen-garden, possessed themselves of the back yard and offices; while a company of skirmishing stoats who stuck at nothing occupied the conservatory and the billiard-room, and held the French windows opening on to the lawn.

"The Mole and the Badger were sitting by the fire in the smoking-room, telling stories and suspecting nothing, for it wasn't a night for any animals to be out in, when those bloodthirsty villains broke down the doors and rushed in

upon them from every side. They made the best fight they could, but what was the good? They were unarmed, and taken by surprise, and what can two animals do against hundreds? They took and beat them severely with sticks, those two poor faithful creatures, and turned them out into the cold and the wet, with many insulting and uncalled-for remarks!"

Here the unfeeling Toad broke into a snigger, and then pulled himself together and tried to look particularly solemn.

"And the Wild Wooders have been living in Toad Hall ever since," continued the Rat; "and going on simply anyhow! Lying in bed half the day, and breakfast at all hours, and the place in such a mess (I'm told) it's not fit to be seen! Eating your grub, and drinking your drink, and making bad jokes about you, and singing vulgar songs, about – well, about prisons and magistrates, and policemen; horrid personal songs, with no humour in them. And they're telling the tradespeople and everybody that they've come to stay for good."

"O, have they!" said Toad getting up and seizing a stick. "I'll jolly soon see about that!"

"It's no good, Toad!" called the Rat after him. "You'd better come back and sit down; you'll only get into trouble."

But the Toad was off, and there was no holding him. He marched rapidly down the road, his stick over his shoulder, fuming and muttering to himself in his anger, till he got near his front gate, when suddenly there popped up from behind the palings a long yellow ferret with a gun.

"Who comes there?" said the ferret sharply.

"Stuff and nonsense!" said Toad, very angrily. "What do you mean by talking like that to me? Come out of it at once, or I'll –"

The ferret said never a word, but he brought his gun up to his shoulder. Toad prudently dropped flat in the road, and *Bang!* a bullet whistled over his head.

The startled Toad scrambled to his feet and scampered off down the road as

hard as he could; and as he ran he heard the ferret laughing and other horrid thin little laughs taking it up and carrying on the sound.

He went back, very crestfallen, and told the Water Rat.

"What did I tell you?" said the Rat. "It's no good. They've got sentries posted, and they are all armed. You must just wait."

Still, Toad was not inclined to give in all at once. So he got out the boat, and set off rowing up the river to where the garden front of Toad Hall came down to the waterside.

Arriving within sight of his old home, he rested on his oars and surveyed the land cautiously. All seemed very peaceful and deserted and quiet. He could see the whole front of Toad Hall, glowing in the evening sunshine, the pigeons settling by twos and threes along the straight line of the roof; the garden, a blaze of flowers; the creek that led up to the boat-house, the little wooden bridge that crossed it; all tranquil, uninhabited, apparently waiting for his return. He would try the boat-house first, he thought. Very warily he paddled up to the mouth of the creek, and was just passing under the bridge, when . . . *Crash!*

A great stone, dropped from above, smashed through the bottom of the boat. It filled and sank, and Toad found himself struggling in deep water. Looking up, he saw two stoats leaning over the parapet of the bridge and watching him with great glee. "It will be your head next time, Toady!" they called out to him. The indignant Toad swam to shore, while the stoats laughed and laughed, supporting each other, and laughed again, till they nearly had two fits – that is, one fit each, of course.

The Toad retraced his weary way on foot, and related his disappointing experiences to the Water Rat once more.

"Well, *what* did I tell you?" said the Rat very crossly. "And, now, look here! See what you've been and done! Lost me my boat that I was so fond of, that's what you've done! And simply ruined that nice suit of clothes that I lent you!

Really, Toad, of all the trying animals – I wonder you manage to keep any friends at all!"

The Toad saw at once how wrongly and foolishly he had acted. He admitted his errors and wrong-headedness and made a full apology to Rat for losing his boat and spoiling his clothes. And he wound up by saying, with that frank self-surrender which always disarmed his friends' criticism and won them back to his side, "Ratty! I see that I have been a headstrong and a wilful Toad! Henceforth, believe me, I will be humble and submissive, and will take no action without your kind advice and full approval!"

"If that is really so," said the good-natured Rat, already appeased, "then my advice to you is, considering the lateness of the hour, to sit down and have your supper, which will be on the table in a minute, and be very patient. For I am convinced that we can do nothing until we have seen the Mole and the Badger, and heard their latest news, and held conference and taken their advice in this difficult matter."

"O, ah, yes, of course, the Mole and the Badger," said Toad, lightly. "What's become of them, the dear fellows? I had forgotten all about them."

"Well may you ask!" said the Rat reproachfully. "While you were riding about the country in expensive motor-cars, and galloping proudly on blood-horses, and breakfasting on the fat of the land, those two poor devoted animals have been camping out in the open, in every sort of weather, living very rough by day and lying very hard by night; watching over your house, patrolling your boundaries, keeping a constant eye on the stoats and weasels, scheming and planning and contriving how to get your property back for you. You don't deserve to have such true and loyal friends, Toad, you don't, really. Some day, when it's too late, you'll be sorry you didn't value them more while you had them!"

"I'm an ungrateful beast, I know," sobbed Toad, shedding bitter tears. "Let me go out and find them, out into the cold, dark night, and share their hardships, and try and prove by – Hold on a bit! Surely I heard the chink of dishes on a tray! Supper's here at last, hooray! Come on, Ratty!"

The Rat remembered that poor Toad had been on prison fare for a considerable time, and that large allowances had therefore to be made. He followed him to the table accordingly, and hospitably encouraged him in his gallant efforts to make up for past privations.

They had just finished their meal and resumed their arm-chairs, when there came a heavy knock at the door.

Toad was nervous, but the Rat, nodding mysteriously at him, went straight up to the door and opened it, and in walked Mr Badger.

He had all the appearance of one who for some nights had been kept away from home and all its little comforts and conveniences. His shoes were covered with mud, and he was looking very rough and tousled; but then he had never been a very smart man, the Badger, at the best of times. He came solemnly up to Toad, shook him by the paw, and said, "Welcome home, Toad! Alas! what am I saying? Home, indeed! This is a poor home-coming. Unhappy Toad!" Then he turned his back on him, sat down to the table, drew his chair up, and helped himself to a large slice of cold pie.

Toad was quite alarmed at this very serious and portentous style of greeting; but the Rat whispered to him, "Never mind; don't take any notice; and don't say anything to him just yet. He's always rather low and despondent when he's wanting his victuals. In half an hour's time he'll be quite a different animal."

So they waited in silence, and presently there came another and a lighter knock. The Rat, with a nod to Toad, went to the door and ushered in the Mole, very shabby and unwashed, with bits of hay and straw sticking in his fur.

"Hooray! Here's old Toad!" cried the Mole, his face beaming. "Fancy having you back again!" And he began to dance round him. "We never dreamt you would turn up so soon! Why, you must have managed to escape, you clever, ingenious, intelligent Toad!"

The Rat, alarmed, pulled him by the elbow; but it was too late. Toad was puffing and swelling already.

"Clever? O, no!" he said. "I'm not really clever, according to my friends. I've only broken out of the strongest prison in England, that's all! And captured a railway train and escaped on it, that's all! And disguised myself and gone about the country humbugging everybody, that's all! O, no! I'm a stupid ass, I am! I'll tell you one or two of my little adventures, Mole, and you shall judge for yourself!"

"Well, well," said the Mole, moving towards the supper-table; "supposing you talk while I eat. Not a bite since breakfast! O my! O my!" And he sat down and helped himself liberally to cold beef and pickles.

Toad straddled on the hearth-rug, thrust his paw into his trouser-pocket and pulled out a handful of silver. "Look at that!" he cried, displaying it. "That's not so bad, is it, for a few minutes' work? And how do you think I done it, Mole? Horse-dealing! That's how I done it!"

"Go on, Toad," said the Mole, immensely interested.

"Toad, do be quiet, please!" said the Rat. "And don't you egg him on, Mole, when you know what he is; but please tell us as soon as possible what the position is, and what's best to be done, now that Toad is back at last."

"The position's about as bad as it can be," replied the Mole grumpily; "and as for what's to be done, why, blest if I know! The Badger and I have been round and round the place, by night and by day; always the same thing. Sentries posted everywhere, guns poked out at us, stones thrown at us; always an animal on the look-out, and when they see us, my! how they do laugh! That's what annoys me most!"

"It's a very difficult situation," said the Rat, reflecting deeply. "But I think I see now, in the depths of my mind, what Toad really ought to do. I will tell you. He ought to –"

"No, he oughtn't!" shouted the Mole, with his mouth full. "Nothing of the sort! You don't understand. What he ought to do is, he ought to –"

"Well, I shan't do it, anyway!" cried Toad, getting excited. "I'm not going to be ordered about by you fellows! It's my house we're talking about, and I know exactly what to do, and I'll tell you. I'm going to –"

By this time they were all three talking at once, at the top of their voices, and the noise was simply deafening, when a thin, dry voice made itself heard, saying "Be quiet at once, all of you!" and instantly everyone was silent.

It was the Badger, who, having finished his pie, had turned round in his chair and was looking at them severely. When he saw that he had secured their attention, and that they were evidently waiting for him to address them, he turned back to the table again and reached out for the cheese. And so great was the respect commanded by the solid qualities of that admirable animal, that not another word was uttered until he had quite finished his repast and brushed the crumbs from his knees. The Toad fidgeted a good deal, but the Rat held him firmly down.

When the Badger had quite done, he got up from his seat and stood before the fireplace, reflecting deeply. At last he spoke.

"Toad!" he said severely. "You bad, troublesome little animal! Aren't you ashamed of yourself? What do you think your father, my old friend, would have said if he had been here tonight, and had known of all your goings on?"

Toad, who was on the sofa by this time, with his legs up, rolled over on his face, shaken by sobs of contrition.

"There, there!" went on the Badger more kindly. "Never mind. Stop crying. We're going to let bygones be bygones, and try and turn over a new leaf. But what the Mole says is quite true. The stoats are on guard, at every point, and they make the best sentinels in the world. It's quite useless to think of attacking the place. They're too strong for us."

"Then it's all over," sobbed the Toad, crying into the sofa cushions. "I shall go and enlist for a soldier, and never see my dear Toad Hall any more!"

"Come, cheer up, Toady!" said the Badger. "There are more ways of getting back a place than taking it by storm. I haven't said my last word yet. Now I'm going to tell you a great secret."

Toad sat up slowly and dried his eyes. Secrets had an immense attraction for him, because he never could keep one, and he enjoyed the sort of unhallowed thrill he experienced when he went and told another animal, after having faithfully promised not to.

"There – is – an – underground – passage," said the Badger, impressively, "that leads from the river bank, quite near here, right up into the middle of Toad Hall."

"O, nonsense! Badger," said Toad, rather airily. "You've been listening to some of the yarns they spin in the public-houses about here. I know every inch of Toad Hall, inside and out. Nothing of the sort, I do assure you!"

"My young friend," said the Badger, with great severity, "your father, who was a worthy animal – a lot worthier than some others I know – was a particular friend of mine, and told me a great deal he wouldn't have dreamt of telling you. He discovered that passage – he didn't make it, of course; that was done hundreds of years before he ever came to live there – and he repaired it and cleaned it out, because he thought it might come in useful some day, in case of trouble or danger; and he showed it to me. 'Don't let my son know about it,' he said. 'He's a good boy, but very light and volatile in character, and simply cannot hold his tongue. If he's ever in a real fix, and it would be of use to him, you may tell him about the secret passage; but not before'."

The other animals looked hard at Toad to see how he would take it. Toad was inclined to be sulky at first; but he brightened up immediately, like the good fellow he was.

"Well, well," he said; "perhaps I am a bit of a talker. A popular fellow such as I am – my friends get round me – we chaff, we sparkle, we tell witty stories – and somehow my tongue gets wagging. I have the gift of conversation. I've been told I ought to have a *salon*, whatever that may be. Never mind. Go on, Badger. How's this passage of yours going to help us?"

"I've found out a thing or two lately," continued the Badger. "I got Otter to disguise himself as a sweep and call at the back door with brushes over his shoulder, asking for a job. There's going to be a big banquet to-morrow night. It's somebody's birthday – the Chief Weasel's, I believe – and all the weasels will be gathered together in the dining-hall, eating and drinking and laughing and carrying on, suspecting nothing. No guns, no swords, no sticks, no arms of any sort whatever!"

"But the sentinels will be posted as usual," remarked the Rat.

"Exactly," said the Badger; "that is my point. The weasels will trust entirely to their excellent sentinels. And that is where the passage comes in. That very useful tunnel leads right up under the butler's pantry, next to the dining-hall!"

"Aha! that squeaky board in the butler's pantry!" said Toad. "Now I understand it!"

"We shall creep out quietly into the butler's pantry –" cried the Mole.

"– with our pistols and swords and sticks –" shouted the Rat.

"– and rush in upon them," said the Badger.

"– and whack 'em, and whack 'em, and whack 'em!" cried the Toad in ecstasy, running round and round the room, and jumping over the chairs.

"Very well, then," said the Badger, resuming his usual dry manner, "our plan is settled, and there's nothing more for you to argue and squabble about. So, as it's getting very late, all of you go right off to bed at once. We will make all the necessary arrangements in the course of the morning to-morrow."

Toad, of course, went off to bed dutifully with the rest – he knew better than to refuse – though he was feeling much too excited to sleep. But he had had a long day, with many events crowded into it; and sheets and blankets were very friendly and comforting things, after plain straw, and not too much of it, spread on the stone floor of a draughty cell; and his head had not been many seconds on his pillow before he was snoring happily. Naturally, he dreamt a good deal; about roads that ran away from him just when he wanted them, and canals that chased him and caught him, and a barge that sailed into the banqueting-hall with his week's washing, just as he was giving a dinner-party; and he was alone in the secret passage, pushing onwards, but it twisted and turned round and shook itself, and sat up on its end; yet somehow, at the last, he found himself back in Toad Hall, safe and triumphant, with all his friends gathered round about him, earnestly assuring him that he really was a clever Toad.

He slept till a late hour next morning, and by the time he got down he found that the other animals had finished their breakfast some time before. The Mole had slipped off somewhere by himself, without telling anyone where he was going to. The Badger sat in the arm-chair, reading the paper, and not concerning himself in the slightest about what was going to happen that very evening. The Rat, on the other hand, was running round the room busily, with his arms full of weapons of every kind, distributing them in four little heaps on the floor, and saying excitedly under his breath, as he ran, "Here's-a-sword-for-the-Rat, here's-a-sword-for-the Mole, here's-a-sword-for-the-Toad, here's-a-sword-for-the-Badger! Here's-a-pistol-for-the-Rat, here's-a-pistol-for-the-Mole, here's-a-pistol-for-the-Toad, here's-a-pistol-for-the-Badger!" And so on, in a regular, rhythmical way, while the four little heaps gradually grew and grew.

"That's all very well, Rat," said the Badger presently, looking at the busy little animal over the edge of his newspaper; "I'm not blaming you. But just let us once get past the stoats, with those detestable guns of theirs, and I assure you we shan't want any swords or pistols. We four, with our sticks, once we're inside the dining-hall, why, we shall clear the floor of all the lot of them in five minutes. I'd have done the whole thing by myself, only I didn't want to deprive you fellows of the fun!"

"It's as well to be on the safe side," said the Rat reflectively, polishing a pistol-barrel on his sleeve and looking along it.

The Toad, having finished his breakfast, picked up a stout stick and swung it vigorously, belabouring imaginary animals. "I'll learn 'em to steal my house!" he cried. "I'll learn 'em, I'll learn 'em!"

"Don't say 'learn 'em', Toad," said the Rat, greatly shocked. "It's not good English."

"What are you always nagging at Toad for?" inquired the Badger rather peevishly. "What's the matter with his English? It's the same what I use myself, and if it's good enough for me, it ought to be good enough for you!"

"I'm very sorry," said the Rat humbly. "Only I *think* it ought to be 'teach 'em', not 'learn 'em'."

"But we don't *want* to teach 'em," replied the Badger. "We want to *learn* 'em – learn 'em, learn 'em! And what's more, we're going to *do* it, too!"

"O, very well, have it your own way," said the Rat. He was getting rather muddled about it himself, and presently he retired into a corner, where he could be heard muttering, "Learn 'em, teach 'em, teach 'em, learn 'em!" till the Badger told him rather sharply to leave off.

Presently the Mole came tumbling into the room, evidently very pleased with himself. "I've been having such fun!" he began at once; "I've been getting a rise out of the stoats!"

"I hope you've been very careful, Mole?" said the Rat anxiously.

"I should hope so, too," said the Mole confidently. "I got the idea when I went into the kitchen, to see about Toad's breakfast being kept hot for him. I found that old washerwoman-dress that he came home in yesterday, hanging on a towel-horse before the fire. So I put it on, and the bonnet as well, and the shawl, and off I went to Toad Hall, as bold as you please. The sentries were on

the look-out, of course, with their guns and their 'who comes there?' and all the rest of their nonsense. 'Good morning, gentlemen!' says I, very respectful. 'Want any washing done to-day?'

"They looked at me very proud and stiff and haughty, and said, 'Go away, washerwoman! We don't do any washing on duty.' 'Or any other time?' says I. Ho, ho, ho! Wasn't I *funny*, Toad?"

"Poor, frivolous animal!" said Toad, very loftily. The fact is, he felt exceedingly jealous of Mole for what he had just done. It was exactly what he would have liked to have done himself, if only he had thought of it first, and hadn't gone and overslept himself.

"Some of the stoats turned quite pink," continued the Mole, "and the sergeant in charge, he said to me, very short, he said, 'Now run away, my good woman, run away! Don't keep my men idling and talking on their posts.' 'Run away?' says I; 'it won't be me that'll be running away, in a very short time from now!' "

"O *Moly*, how could you?" said the Rat, dismayed.

The Badger laid down his paper.

"I could see them pricking up their ears and looking at each other," went on the Mole; "and the Sergeant said to them, 'Never mind *her*; she doesn't know what she's talking about.'

" 'O! don't I?' said I. 'Well, let me tell you this. My daughter, she washes for Mr Badger, and that'll show you whether I know what I'm talking about; and *you'll* know pretty soon, too! A hundred bloodthirsty Badgers, armed with rifles, are going to attack Toad Hall this very night, by way of the paddock. Six boat-loads of Rats, with pistols and cutlasses, will come up the river and effect a landing in the garden; while a picked body of Toads, known as the Die-hards, or the Death-or-Glory Toads, will storm the orchard and carry everything before them, yelling for vengeance. There won't be much left of you to wash, by the time they've done with you, unless you clear out while you have the chance!' Then I ran away, and when I was out of sight I hid; and presently I came creeping back along the ditch and took a peep at them through the hedge. They were all as nervous and flustered as could be, running all ways at once, and falling over each other, and everyone giving orders to everybody else and not listening; and the sergeant kept sending off parties of stoats to distant parts of the grounds, and then sending other fellows to fetch 'em back again; and I heard them saying to each other, 'That's *just* like the weasels; they're to stop comfortably in the banqueting-hall, and have feasting and toasts and songs and all sorts of fun, while we must stay on guard in the cold and the dark, and in the end be cut to pieces by bloodthirsty Badgers!' "

"O, you silly ass, Mole!" cried Toad. "You've been and spoilt everything!"

"Mole," said the Badger, in his dry, quiet way, "I perceive you have more sense in your little finger than some other animals have in the whole of their fat bodies. You have managed excellently, and I begin to have great hopes of you. Good Mole! Clever Mole!"

The Toad was simply wild with jealousy, more especially as he couldn't make out for the life of him what the Mole had done that was so particularly clever; but, fortunately for him, before he could show temper or expose himself to the Badger's sarcasm, the bell rang for luncheon.

It was a simple but sustaining meal – bacon and broad beans, and a macaroni pudding; and when they had quite done, the Badger settled himself into an arm-chair, and said, "Well, we've got our work cut out for us to-night, and it will probably be pretty late before we're quite through with it; so I'm just going to take forty winks, while I can." And he drew a handkerchief over his face and was soon snoring.

The anxious and laborious Rat at once resumed his preparations, and started running between his four little heaps, muttering, "Here's-a-belt-for-the-

Rat, here's-a-belt-for-the Mole, here's-a-belt-for-the-Toad, here's-a-belt-for-the-Badger!" and so on, with every fresh accoutrement he produced, to which there seemed really no end; so the Mole drew his arm through Toad's, led him out into the open air, shoved him into a wicker chair, and made him tell him all his adventures from beginning to end, which Toad was only too willing to do. The Mole was a good listener, and Toad, with no one to check his statements or to criticize in an unfriendly spirit, rather let himself go. Indeed, much that he related belonged more properly to the category of what-might-have-happened-had-I-only-thought-of-it-in-time-instead-of-ten-minutes-afterwards. Those are always the best and the raciest adventures; and why should they not be truly ours, as much as the somewhat inadequate things that really come off?

Chapter 12

The Return of Ulysses

When it began to grow dark, the Rat, with an air of excitement and mystery, summoned them back into the parlour, stood each of them up alongside of his little heap, and proceeded to dress them up for the coming expedition. He was very earnest and thoroughgoing about it, and the affair took quite a long time. First, there was a belt to go round each animal, and then a sword to be stuck into each belt, and then a cutlass on the other side to balance it. Then a pair of pistols, a policeman's truncheon, several sets of handcuffs, some bandages and sticking-plaster, and a flask and a sandwich-case. The Badger laughed good-humouredly and said, "All right, Ratty! It amuses you and it doesn't hurt me. I'm going to do all I've got to do

with this here stick." But the Rat only said, "*Please*, Badger. You know I shouldn't like you to blame me afterwards and say I had forgotten *anything*!"

When all was quite ready, the Badger took a dark lantern in one paw, grasped his great stick with the other, and said, "Now then, follow me! Mole first, 'cos I'm very pleased with him; Rat next; Toad last. And look here, Toady! Don't you chatter so much as usual, or you'll be sent back, as sure as fate!"

The Toad was so anxious not to be left out that he took up the inferior position assigned to him without a murmur, and the animals set off. The Badger led them along by the river for a little way, and then suddenly swung himself over the edge into a hole in the river bank, a little above the water. The Mole and the Rat followed silently, swinging themselves successfully into the hole as they had seen the Badger do; but when it came to Toad's turn, of course, he managed to slip and fall into the water with a loud splash and a squeal of alarm. He was hauled out by his friends, rubbed down and wrung out hastily, comforted, and set on his legs; but the Badger was seriously angry, and told him that the very next time he made a fool of himself he would most certainly be left behind.

So at last they were in the secret passage, and the cutting-out expedition had really begun!

It was cold, and dark, and damp, and low, and narrow, and poor Toad began to shiver, partly from dread of what might be before him, partly because he was wet through. The lantern was far ahead, and he could not help lagging behind a little in the darkness. Then he heard the Rat call out warningly, "*Come* on, Toad!" and a terror seized him of being left behind, alone in the darkness, and he came on with such a rush that he upset the Rat into the Mole and the Mole into the Badger, and for a moment all was confusion. The Badger thought they were being attacked from behind, and, as there was no room to use a stick or a cutlass, drew a pistol, and was on the point of putting a bullet into

Toad. When he found out what had really happened he was very angry indeed, and said, "Now this time that tiresome Toad *shall* be left behind!"

But Toad whimpered, and the other two promised that they would be answerable for his good conduct, and at last the Badger was pacified, and the procession moved on; only this time the Rat brought up the rear, with a firm grip on the shoulder of Toad.

So they groped and shuffled along, with their ears pricked up and their paws on their pistols, till at last the Badger said, "We ought by now to be pretty nearly under the Hall."

Then suddenly they heard, far away as it might be, and yet apparently nearly over their heads, a confused murmur of sound, as if people were shouting and cheering and stamping on the floor and hammering on tables. The Toad's nervous terrors all returned, but the Badger only remarked placidly, "They *are* going it, the weasels!"

The passage now began to slope upwards; they groped onward a little further, and then the noise broke out again, quite distinct this time, and very close above them. "Oo-ray-oo-ray-oo-ray-ooray!" they heard, and the stamping of little feet on the floor, and the clinking of glasses as little fists pounded on the table. "*What* a time they're having!" said the Badger. "Come on!" They hurried along the passage till it came to a full stop, and they found themselves standing under the trap-door that led up into the butler's pantry. Such a tremendous noise was going on in the banqueting-hall that there was little danger of their being overheard. The Badger said, "Now, boys, all together!" and the four of them put their shoulders to the trap-door and heaved it back. Hoisting each other up, they found themselves standing in the pantry, with only a door between them and the banqueting-hall, where their unconscious enemies were carousing.

The noise, as they emerged from the passage, was simply deafening. At last, as the cheering and hammering slowly subsided, a voice could be made out saying, "Well, I do not propose to detain you much longer"– (great applause) – "but before I resume my seat"– (renewed cheering) – "I should like to say one word about our kind host, Mr Toad. We all know Toad!"– (great laughter) – "*Good* Toad, *modest* Toad, *honest* Toad!" (shrieks of merriment).

"Only just let me get at him!" muttered Toad, grinding his teeth.

"Hold hard a minute!" said the Badger, restraining him with difficulty. "Get ready, all of you!"

"– Let me sing you a little song," went on the voice, "which I have composed on the subject of Toad"– (prolonged applause).

Then the Chief Weasel – for it was he – began in a high, squeaky voice –

"Toad he went a-pleasuring
 Gaily down the street –"

The Badger drew himself up, took a firm grip of his stick with both paws, glanced round at his comrades, and cried –

"The hour is come! Follow me!"

And flung the door wide open.

My!

What a squealing and a squeaking and a screeching filled the air!

Well might the terrified weasels dive under the tables and spring madly up at the windows! Well might the ferrets rush wildly for the fireplace and get hopelessly jammed in the chimney! Well might tables and chairs be upset, and glass and china be sent crashing on the floor, in the panic of that terrible moment when the four Heroes strode wrathfully into the room! The mighty Badger, his whiskers bristling, his great cudgel whistling through the air; Mole, black and grim, brandishing his stick and shouting his awful war-cry, "A Mole!

A Mole!" Rat, desperate and determined, his belt bulging with weapons of every age and every variety; Toad, frenzied with excitement and injured pride, swollen to twice his ordinary size, leaping into the air and emitting Toad-whoops that chilled them to the marrow! "Toad he went a-pleasuring!" he yelled. "I'll pleasure 'em!" and he went straight for the Chief Weasel. They were but four in all, but to the panic-stricken weasels the hall seemed full of monstrous animals, grey, black, brown and yellow, whooping and flourishing enormous cudgels; and they broke and fled with squeals of terror and dismay, this way and that, through the windows, up the chimney, anywhere to get out of reach of those terrible sticks.

The affair was soon over. Up and down, the whole length of the hall, strode the four Friends, whacking with their sticks at every head that showed itself; and in five minutes the room was cleared. Through the broken windows the shrieks of terrified weasels escaping across the lawn were borne faintly to their ears; on the floor lay prostrate some dozen or so of the enemy, on whom the

Mole was busily engaged in fitting handcuffs. The Badger, resting from his labours, leant on his stick and wiped his honest brow.

"Mole," he said, "you're the best of fellows! Just cut along outside and look after those stoat-sentries of yours, and see what they're doing. I've an idea that, thanks to you, we shan't have much trouble from *them* to-night!"

The Mole vanished promptly through a window; and the Badger bade the other two set a table on its legs again, pick up knives and forks and plates and glasses from the débris on the floor, and see if they could find materials for a supper. "I want some grub, I do," he said, in that rather common way he had of speaking. "Stir your stumps, Toad, and look lively! We've got your house back for you, and you don't offer us so much as a sandwich."

Toad felt rather hurt that the Badger didn't say pleasant things to him, as he had to the Mole, and tell him what a fine fellow he was, and how splendidly he had fought; for he was rather particularly pleased with himself and the way he had gone for the Chief Weasel and sent him flying across the table with one blow of his stick. But he bustled about, and so did the Rat, and soon they found some guava jelly in a glass dish, and a cold chicken, a tongue that had hardly been touched, some trifle, and quite a lot of lobster salad; and in the pantry they came upon a basketful of French rolls and any quantity of cheese, butter, and celery. They were just about to sit down when the Mole clambered in through the window, chuckling, with an armful of rifles.

"It's all over," he reported. "From what I can make out, as soon as the stoats, who were very nervous and jumpy already, heard the shrieks and the yells and the uproar inside the hall, some of them threw down their rifles and fled. The others stood fast for a bit, but when the weasels came rushing out upon them they thought they were betrayed; and the stoats grappled with the weasels, and the weasels fought to get away, and they wrestled and wriggled and punched each other, and rolled over and over, till most of 'em rolled into the river! They've all disappeared by now, one way or another; and I've got their rifles. So *that's* all right!"

"Excellent and deserving animal!" said the Badger, his mouth full of chicken and trifle. "Now, there's just one more thing I want you to do, Mole, before you sit down to your supper along of us; and I wouldn't trouble you only I know I can trust you to see a thing done, and I wish I could say the same of everyone I know. I'd send Rat, if he wasn't a poet. I want you to take those fellows on the floor there upstairs with you, and have some bedrooms cleaned out and tidied up and made really comfortable. See that they sweep *under* the beds, and put clean sheets and pillow-cases on, and turn down one corner of the bed-clothes, just as you know it ought to be done; and have a can of hot water, and clean towels, and fresh cakes of soap, put in each room. And then you can give them a licking a-piece, if it's any satisfaction to you, and put them out by the back door, and we shan't see any more of *them*, I fancy. And then come along and have some of this cold tongue. It's first rate. I'm very pleased with you, Mole!"

The good-natured Mole picked up a stick, formed his prisoners up in a line on the floor, gave them the order "Quick march!" and led his squad off to the upper floor. After a time, he appeared again, smiling, and said that every room was ready, and as clean as a new pin. "And I didn't have to lick them, either," he added. "I thought, on the whole, they had had licking enough for one night, and the weasels, when I put the point to them, quite agreed with me, and said they wouldn't think of troubling me. They were very penitent, and said they were extremely sorry for what they had done, but it was all the fault of the Chief Weasel and the stoats, and if ever they could do anything for us at any time to make up, we had only got to mention it. So

I gave them a roll apiece, and let them out at the back, and off they ran, as hard as they could!"

Then the Mole pulled his chair up to the table, and pitched into the cold tongue; and Toad, like the gentleman he was, put all his jealousy from him, and said heartily, "Thank you kindly, dear Mole, for all your pains and trouble to-night, and especially for your cleverness this morning!" The Badger was pleased at that, and said, "There spoke my brave Toad!" So they finished their supper in great joy and contentment, and presently retired to rest between clean sheets, safe in Toad's ancestral home, won back by matchless valour, consummate strategy, and a proper handling of sticks.

The following morning, Toad, who had overslept himself as usual, came down to breakfast disgracefully late, and found on the table a certain quantity of egg-shells, some fragments of cold and leathery toast, a coffee-pot three-fourths empty, and really very little else; which did not tend to improve his temper, considering that, after all, it was his own house. Through the French windows of the breakfast-room he could see the Mole and the Water Rat sitting in wicker-chairs out on the lawn, evidently telling each other stories; roaring with laughter and kicking their short legs up in the air. The Badger, who was in an arm-chair and deep in the morning paper, merely looked up and nodded when Toad entered the room. But Toad knew his man, so he sat down and made the best breakfast he could, merely observing to himself that he would get square with the others sooner or later. When he had nearly finished, the Badger looked up and remarked rather shortly: "I'm sorry, Toad, but I'm afraid there's a heavy morning's work in front of you. You see, we really ought to have a Banquet at once, to celebrate this affair. It's expected of you – in fact, it's the rule."

"O, all right!" said the Toad, readily. "Anything to oblige. Though why on earth you should want to have a Banquet in the morning I cannot understand. But you know I do not live to please myself, but merely to find out what my friends want, and then try and arrange it for 'em, you dear old Badger!"

"Don't pretend to be stupider than you really are," replied the Badger, crossly; "and don't chuckle and splutter in your coffee while you're talking; it's not manners. What I mean is, the Banquet will be at night, of course, but the invitations will have to be written and got off at once, and you've got to write 'em. Now, sit down at that table – there's stacks of letter-paper on it, with 'Toad Hall' at the top in blue and gold – and write invitations to all our friends, and if you stick to it we shall get them out before luncheon. And *I'll* bear a hand, too; and take my share of the burden. *I'll* order the Banquet."

"What!" cried Toad, dismayed. "Me stop indoors and write a lot of rotten letters on a jolly morning like this, when I want to go around my property, and set everything and everybody to rights, and swagger about and enjoy myself! Certainly not! I'll be – I'll see you – Stop a minute, though! Why, of course, dear Badger! What is my pleasure or convenience compared with that of others? You wish it done, and it shall be done. Go, Badger, order the Banquet, order what you like; then join our young friends outside in their innocent mirth, oblivious of me and my cares and toils. I sacrifice this fair morning on the altar of duty and friendship!"

The Badger looked at him very suspiciously, but Toad's frank, open countenance made it difficult to suggest any unworthy motive in this change of attitude. He quitted the room, accordingly, in the direction of the kitchen, and as soon as the door had closed behind him, Toad hurried to the writing-table. A fine idea had occurred to him while he was talking. He *would* write the invitations; and he would take care to mention the leading part he had taken in the fight, and how he had laid the Chief Weasel flat; and he would hint at his adventures, and what a career of triumph he had to tell about; and on the fly-leaf he would set out a sort of a programme of entertainment for the evening – something like this, as he sketched it out in his head:

SPEECH . . . . BY TOAD
(There will be other speeches by TOAD
during the evening)

ADDRESS . . . . . . BY TOAD
SYNOPSIS – Our Prison System – The
Waterways of Old England – Horse-
dealing, and how to deal – Property, its
rights and its duties – Back to the Land –
A Typical English Squire.

SONG . . . . BY TOAD
(*Composed by himself*)

OTHER COMPOSITIONS . . BY TOAD
will be sung in the course of the
evening by the . . . COMPOSER.

The idea pleased him mightily, and he worked very hard and got all the letters finished by noon, at which hour it was reported to him that there was a small and rather bedraggled weasel at the door, inquiring timidly whether he could be of any service to the gentlemen. Toad swaggered out and found it was one of the prisoners of the previous evening, very respectful and anxious to please. He patted him on the head, shoved the bundle of invitations into his paw, and told him to cut along quick and deliver them as fast as he could, and if he liked to come back again in the evening, perhaps there might be a shilling for him, or, again, perhaps there mightn't; and the poor weasel seemed really quite grateful, and hurried off eagerly to do his mission.

When the other animals came back to luncheon, very boisterous and breezy after a morning on the river, the Mole, whose conscience had been pricking him, looked doubtfully at Toad, expecting to find him sulky or depressed. Instead, he was so uppish and inflated that the Mole began to suspect something; while the Rat and the Badger exchanged significant glances.

As soon as the meal was over, Toad thrust his paws deep into his trouser-pockets, remarked casually, "Well, look after yourselves, you fellows! Ask for anything you want!" and was swaggering off in the direction of the garden, where he wanted to think out an idea or two for his coming speeches, when the Rat caught him by the arm.

Toad rather suspected what he was after, and did his best to get away; but when the Badger took him firmly by the other arm he began to see that the game was up. The two animals conducted him between them into the small smoking-room that opened out of the entrance-hall, shut the door, and put him into a chair.

Then they both stood in front of him, while Toad sat silent and regarded them with much suspicion and ill-humour.

"Now, look here, Toad," said the Rat. "It's about this Banquet, and very sorry I am to have to speak to you like this. But we want you to understand clearly, once and for all, that there are going to be no speeches and no songs. Try and grasp the fact that on this occasion we're not arguing with you; we're just telling you."

Toad saw that he was trapped. They understood him, they saw through him, they had got ahead of him. His pleasant dream was shattered.

"Mayn't I sing them just one *little* song?" he pleaded piteously.

"No, not *one* little song," replied the Rat firmly, though his heart bled as he noticed the trembling lip of the poor disappointed Toad. "It's no good, Toady;

you know well that your songs are all conceit and boasting and vanity; and your speeches are all self-praise and – and – well, and gross exaggeration and – and –"

"And gas," put in the Badger, in his common way.

"It's for your own good, Toady," went on the Rat. "You know you *must* turn over a new leaf sooner or later, and now seems a splendid time to begin; a sort of turning-point in your career. Please don't think that saying all this doesn't hurt me more than it hurts you."

Toad remained a long while plunged in thought. At last he raised his head, and the traces of strong emotion were visible on his features. "You have conquered, my friends," he said in broken accents. "It was, to be sure, but a small thing that I asked – merely leave to blossom and expand for yet one more evening, to let myself go and hear the tumultuous applause that always seems to me – somehow – to bring out my best qualities. However, you are right, I know, and I am wrong. Henceforth I will be a very different Toad. My friends, you shall never have occasion to blush for me again. But, O dear, O dear, this is a hard world!"

And, pressing his handkerchief to his face, he left the room, with faltering footsteps.

"Badger," said the Rat, "*I* feel like a brute; I wonder what *you* feel like?"

"O, I know, I know," said the Badger gloomily. "But the thing had to be done. This good fellow has got to live here, and hold his own, and be respected. Would you have him a common laughing-stock, mocked and jeered at by stoats and weasels?"

"Of course not," said the Rat. "And, talking of weasels, it's lucky we came upon that little weasel, just as he was setting out with Toad's invitations. I suspected something from what you told me, and had a look at one or two; they were simply disgraceful. I confiscated the lot, and the good Mole is now sitting in the blue *boudoir*, filling up plain, simple invitation cards."

At last the hour for the Banquet began to draw near, and Toad, who on leaving the others had retired to his bedroom, was still sitting there, melancholy and thoughtful. His brow resting on his paw, he pondered long and deeply. Gradually his countenance cleared, and he began to smile long, slow smiles. Then he took to giggling in a shy, self-conscious manner. At last he got up, locked the door, drew the curtains across the windows, collected all the chairs in the room and arranged them in a semicircle, and took up his position in front of them, swelling visibly. Then he bowed, coughed twice, and, letting himself go,

with uplifted voice he sang, to the enraptured audience that his imagination so clearly saw:

TOAD'S LAST LITTLE SONG!

The Toad – came – home!
There was panic in the parlour and howling in the hall,
There was crying in the cow-shed and shrieking in the stall,
When the Toad – came – home!

When the Toad – came – home!
There was smashing in of window and crashing in of door,
There was chivvying of weasels that fainted on the floor,
When the Toad – came – home!

Bang! go the drums!
The trumpeters are tooting and the soldiers are saluting,
And the cannon they are shooting and the motor-cars are
hooting,
As the – Hero – comes!

Shout – Hooray!
And let each one of the crowd try and shout it very loud,
In honour of an animal of whom you're justly proud,
For it's Toad's – great – day!

He sang this very loud, with great unction and expression; and when he had done, he sang it all over again.

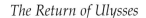

Then he heaved a deep sigh; a long, long, long sigh.

Then he dipped his hairbrush in the water-jug, parted his hair in the middle, and plastered it down very straight and sleek on each side of his face; and, unlocking the door, went quietly down the stairs to greet his guests, who he knew must be assembling in the drawing-room.

All the animals cheered when he entered, and crowded round to congratulate him and say nice things about his courage, and his cleverness, and his fighting qualities; but Toad only smiled faintly, and murmured, "Not at all!" Or, sometimes, for a change, "On the contrary!" Otter, who was standing on the hearthrug, describing to an admiring circle of friends exactly how he would have managed things had he been there, came forward with a shout, threw his arm round Toad's neck, and tried to take him round the room in triumphal progress; but Toad, in a mild way, was rather snubby to him, remarking gently, as he disengaged himself, "Badger's was the master-mind; the Mole and the Water Rat bore the brunt of the fighting; I merely served in the ranks and did little or nothing." The animals were evidently puzzled and taken aback by this unexpected attitude of his; and Toad felt, as he moved from one guest to the other, making his modest responses, that he was an object of absorbing interest to everyone.

The Badger had ordered everything of the best, and the Banquet was a great success. There was much talking and laughter and chaff among the animals, but through it all Toad, who of course was in the chair, looked down his nose and murmured pleasant nothings to the animals on either side of him. At intervals he stole a glance at the Badger and the Rat, and always when he looked they were staring at each other with their mouths open; and this gave him the greatest satisfaction. Some of the younger and livelier animals, as the evening wore on, got whispering to each other that things were not so amusing as they used to be in the good old days; and there were some knockings on the table and cries of "Toad! Speech! Speech from Toad! Song! Mr Toad's Song!" But Toad only shook his head gently, raised one paw in mild protest, and, by pressing delicacies on his guests, by topical small-talk, and by earnest inquiries after members of their families not yet old enough to appear at social functions, managed to convey to them that this dinner was being run on strictly conventional lines.

He was indeed an altered Toad!

After this climax, the four animals continued to lead their lives, so rudely broken in upon by civil war, in great joy and contentment, undisturbed by further risings or invasions. Toad, after due consultation with his friends, selected a handsome gold chain and locket set with pearls, which he dispatched to the gaoler's daughter with a letter that even the Badger admitted to be modest, grateful, and appreciative; and the engine-driver, in his turn, was properly thanked and compensated for all his pains and trouble. Under severe compulsion from the Badger, even the barge-woman was, with some trouble, sought out and the value of her horse discreetly made good to her; though Toad kicked terribly at this, holding himself to be an instrument of Fate, sent to punish fat women with mottled arms who couldn't tell a real gentleman when they saw one. The amount involved, it was true, was not very burdensome, the gipsy's valuation being admitted by local assessors to be approximately correct.

Sometimes, in the course of long summer evenings, the friends would take a stroll together in the Wild Wood, now successfully tamed so far as they were concerned; and it was pleasing to see how respectfully they were greeted by the inhabitants, and how the mother-weasels would bring their young ones to the mouths of their holes, and say, pointing, "Look, baby! There goes the great Mr Toad! And that's the gallant Water Rat, a terrible fighter, walking along o' him! And yonder comes the famous Mr Mole, of whom you so often have heard your father tell!" But when their infants were fractious and quite beyond control, they would quiet them by telling how, if they didn't hush them and not fret them, the terrible grey Badger would up and get them. This was a base libel on Badger, who, though he cared little about society, was rather fond of children; but it never failed to have its full effect.